THE GHOST OF CHRISTMAS PAST

ANGIE FOX

ALSO BY ANGIE FOX

THE SOUTHERN GHOST HUNTER SERIES

Southern Spirits

A Ghostly Gift (short story)

The Skeleton in the Closet

Ghost of a Chance (short story)

The Haunted Heist

Deader Homes & Gardens

Dog Gone Ghost (short story)

Sweet Tea and Spirits

Murder on the Sugarland Express

Pecan Pies and Dead Guys

The Mint Julep Murders

The Ghost of Christmas Past

Southern Bred and Dead

THE ACCIDENTAL DEMON SLAYER SERIES

The Accidental Demon Slayer

The Dangerous Book for Demon Slayers

A Tale of Two Demon Slayers

The Last of the Demon Slayers

My Big Fat Demon Slayer Wedding

Beverly Hills Demon Slayer

Night of the Living Demon Slayer

What To Expect When Your Demon Slayer is Expecting

SHORT STORY COLLECTIONS:

A Little Night Magic: A collection of Southern Ghost Hunter and Accidental Demon Slayer short stories

The Ghost of Christmas Past

NEW YORK *TIMES* BESTSELLING AUTHOR

ANGIE FOX

This edition published by arrangement with Moose Island Publishing.

The Ghost of Christmas Past

First Edition

ISBN: 978-1-939661-61-6

I

The hardest part about stringing Christmas lights on the marble mantel over my fireplace was getting them to stay where I wanted them.

"Halt!" I ordered as the twinkling red and white candy cane lights slid off the far side of the mantel. Perhaps I'd overdone it earlier with the marble polish.

I took a deep breath—not too deep, since I didn't want to test the seams of my party dress—bent down, grabbed the strand, and straightened back up, all without a single wobble. Well, praise be and hallelujah. I was getting the hang of balancing in these heels, at least.

I'd set aside a small budget for holiday decorations this year. It wasn't much—I was still very cautious about spending any of my hard-earned savings after nearly losing the house. But when I'd happened upon a little pop-up holiday store downtown called A Light To Remember, I couldn't resist.

Not only had I found the mantel lights, but also the perfect multicolored net lights for the hydrangea bushes out front. They spot-on matched the plastic balls embedded in the pretty little wreath my mother had sent when she visited Santa Claus, Indiana. The icicle lights went up on the shed, where my ghost friend Frankie had insisted he needed "mood lighting" for his upcoming date with his ghostly girlfriend, Molly. I resisted any and all jokes about his icy touch, his cold gangster heart, or the fact that as the dominant ghost of the shed, he could have conjured up a set of ghostly lights himself.

After all, it was Christmas. And I could certainly spare some holiday cheer.

This string of lights brought that spirit of the holidays to my mantel. Or they would, as soon as I could get them to drape a little without pulling the whole shebang over the edge. I pushed and bunched and arranged the twinkling candy canes a few more times before I remembered the roll of double-sided tape in my kitchen junk drawer. I turned to go get it, and my ankle snagged against something warm and fluffy.

"Whoops!" I managed three staggered steps and some ungraceful pinwheeling of my arms before I found my balance. "Lucille Desiree Long," I chided as my pet skunk snuffled around my ankles, happily oblivious to the disaster she'd almost caused. "You should know better than to sneak up on me like that." Especially when I was wearing heels two inches taller than any woman should and a dress not designed for gymnastics.

My sister, Melody, had lent me the whole kit and caboodle and assured me it was the latest thing. The sleek, sequined dress hugged my curves all the way down to my knees and sparkled like sunrise over a lake. I'd flat-ironed the ever-present wave out of my hair and pinned it back in a high, elegant bun. My makeup was nice but subtle—eyeliner and mascara, a touch of blush and a bright pink shade of lip gloss that I saved for special occasions.

"Christmas with the Wydells," Melody had said with a whistle when I told her why I needed the dress. "I don't envy you."

"It's going to go fine," I'd assured her, and I think we both hoped I wasn't lying through my teeth.

I sighed and swept an errant hair off my face. I was a Southern girl. Practical. Just because the town matriarch, Virginia Wydell, had tried to ruin me and take my ancestral home didn't mean I couldn't spend Christmas with her. I fought the urge to chew at my freshly glossed lips. That sounded bad, even in my head.

Still, I had to find a way to get along with Virginia. I was currently dating one of her sons.

"We'll work it out. We've been making progress," I reminded my little skunk—and myself—as I reached down to stroke Lucy's stubby ears, one of which had turned inside out. After all, I had been invited to this year's Christmas. That hadn't happened in a while.

I straightened up and headed into the kitchen to look for the tape.

Being invited to the Wydell family Christmas party was a big step forward in my relationship with the family. Virginia and I had both been in denial lately about how serious I was becoming about Ellis Wydell. He was the middle of Virginia's three sons, a deputy sheriff for the town of Sugarland, Tennessee, and the most wonderful man I'd ever met. The problem was, he wasn't the first Wydell boy I'd dated.

Years ago I'd been engaged to Ellis's younger brother, Beau. I'd been all set to say, "I do," until Beau hit on my sister the night before the wedding. Needless to say, I'd called it off —but Virginia still stuck me with the bill and ruined my reputation in town.

"But it didn't ruin you and me, did it?" I cooed at Lucy

while I opened the junk drawer. "No, baby girl, it did not." I'd reassembled the scattered pieces of my life, found work again —very challenging work, but ghost hunting was finally paying the bills—and now I was going to celebrate Christmas with Ellis at his cousin Montgomery's house.

Montgomery was his dad's cousin, and one of the stalwart leaders of the family. The last time I'd been to his Christmas party, I was Beau's fiancée. *Don't think about that.* Montgomery Wydell knew how to throw one heck of a celebration. There would be eggnog and roasted chestnuts and—

"Aha!" I found the tape and carried it back out to the fireplace. I tore some pieces off, then arranged my candy cane lights to dangle and dip as I saw fit. A minute later, I stepped back and admired my handiwork. "What do you think, Lucy?"

Her cold nose nudged my ankle. Risking life and limb, I bent again and picked her up to cuddle close to my chest.

Lucy grunted and licked my chin. "I think it's pretty, too," I agreed.

I fingered the gold filigree cross that rested against my throat. It had been my grandmother's, but I'd had to sell it to Virginia Wydell as part of my desperate effort to save my home. I'd only recently gotten it back from her, and now I almost never took it off.

It was proof positive that things could and did sometimes work out.

Tonight was Christmas Eve, a time for family, food, and friendship. Ellis had already texted to let me know he was on the way to pick me up. He'd even punctuated the text with a party-hat emoji, not typical for a man who was mostly accustomed to writing formal reports for the police.

I headed toward the fridge to fetch the ham and cream cheese roll-ups I'd made for the party. It was my grandma's special recipe, with a fresh dill pickle in the middle to make them crisp and delicious.

Despite Virginia Wydell's shortcomings, family meant a lot to Ellis. He loved them and me and wanted to bring us all together at last. It warmed my heart just thinking about it.

I wanted Ellis in every part of my life...even the parts it turned out he really didn't like, like the ghost hunting. I popped open the fridge, adjusted the snowflake-patterned Saran Wrap covering my appetizers, and slid the chilly tray onto one hand like a cocktail waitress.

It had taken me a while to get used to ghost hunting. I hadn't planned to see spirits; I certainly didn't grow up with "the gift." But during my almost-move, when I'd relocated a particularly ugly vase from the attic to the parlor, I'd set a few things in motion that no one could have predicted.

I mean, how was I supposed to know the vase was, in fact, an urn—or that it belonged to a 1920s gangster? Or that I'd trapped him on my property after rinsing the ashy bits out of the urn and into my rosebush? Frankie hadn't spoken up until after the deed was done.

Poor Frankie.

I looked to the trash can by the mantel, where we kept the rosebush and his dirt with the ashes. I'd wrapped it in a festive red ribbon, not that Frankie had noticed.

We hadn't been able to free him yet, but we had done a lot of other things together. My resident ghost could tune me into the other side. It was often scary and dangerous, but always enlightening. I'd solved several mysteries and helped people fix problems that had weighed on them for generations. Ghosts were people too, and they deserved peace just as much as everybody else.

I placed the ham and cheese roll-ups on the mantel and straightened the bow on Frankie's trash can. Next year, I'd buy some lights for his rosebush. Ellis would get a kick out of that, even if he wished Frankie and I would find a new way to occupy our time.

It wasn't enough for Ellis that we were good at ghost hunting, that we helped people. He saw the danger and the fact that anything could happen. It scared him because he loved me, and he couldn't protect me from what he couldn't see or feel in real life. But I couldn't—wouldn't—let fear guide my choices.

Ellis and I needed to talk about it. He still didn't know I'd heard him confessing his fears to Frankie during our last big adventure, and I wasn't sure how he'd take getting called on it. But that could wait until after Christmas.

There was a brisk rap-rap at the door, and Lucy squirmed in my arms as soon as she heard it. I set her down, and she took off at a rapid waddle. I smiled as I followed her. Lucy liked Ellis almost as much as I did. I couldn't wait to see him all decked out in his best outfit instead of in his usual uniform or his jeans and T-shirts. He was handsome either way, of course, but there was something about Ellis Wydell in a suit that made me want to be on the naughty list.

I opened the door with a grin. "Don't you look all—" My voice died abruptly in my throat as I realized it wasn't Ellis at the front door. Just a deliveryman wearing an expression of forced cheer and a hat that read Jackson Orchard Co-op. He held a white plastic clipboard in his hands. "Miss Long?" he asked.

"Yes, that's me," I said, shivering against the cold gusting in through the open door.

"Great." He stepped aside so I could get a better look at what he'd brought. On the porch just behind him was a wicker basket about two feet across at the bottom, filled with a carefully stacked pyramid of beautiful silver and gold foil-wrapped pears. Including the bow-crowned top, the arrangement stood half as tall as I did.

The deliveryman handed over an envelope with a holly berry border as he tried not to stare at Lucy, who was sniffing with great interest at the nearest pear. "From Virginia Wydell."

A present from...Virginia? I pressed the card to my chest as I took in the splendor of the arrangement. It was...I had... "My goodness, how very kind of her," I managed after a moment. It was more than kind, though. This gift was unprecedented. She had never given me anything before, not even when I was engaged to Beau.

I'd only gotten my grandmother's necklace back from her because she'd felt she needed to bribe me to help her out.

This, though, this was the true spirit of Christmas at work. The pears were such a thoughtful gift. I loved fruit, and Lucy loved it even more, and our blueberry patch wasn't producing right now, so it had actually been a while since we'd had something as fresh and appealing as these.

"Will you be paying by cash or check, Miss Long?"

I blinked and took my attention away from the sparkling pyramid, back to the deliveryman. "I'm sorry, what?"

"The balance for the basket is due upon delivery, miss."

How strange. Virginia wasn't one to forget an important detail like that. I managed a smile. Perhaps there was an extra charge for delivering on Christmas Eve. I surely wouldn't mention it. It would only embarrass her. "Yes, of course. How much is delivery?" I asked.

"I'm talking about the balance due for the basket, miss." The deliveryman, first name Brian according to his name tag, handed over his clipboard. On it was a white printout with Jackson Orchard's logo on the top, a description of the basket on the left side, and on the right side, a column titled "Price" that came to a total of...

"One hundred and seventy-two dollars!" I blurted. It was all I could do to stay on my teetering heels. One hundred and seventy-two dollars? For a basket of pears? Did they come straight from the Garden of Eden? "Are you sure this is right?"

"It's the standard price for this particular arrangement," Brian confirmed.

Surely there had to be some mistake. There had to be a note of some kind, or a message from Virginia explaining things. I remembered the little envelope in my hand and ripped it open. The card, beautifully embossed with the same holly berry design, did indeed contain a note from Virginia.

Dearest Verity,

I'm sure you would like to make a good impression tonight, so in the spirit of Christmas I have taken care of your hostess gift for the party. Bring this lovely arrangement and it will at least appear as if you belong.

Best,

Virginia Wydell

2

My face went numb and my brain froze as if the only help my nerves could give me at the moment was to take away all feeling so I didn't have to process what just happened. The edges of the card creased as my grip tightened, and even though I knew I should look away from the note, I couldn't. It was like being in a train wreck—worse, actually, because I was in a train wreck once, and even with the engine careening toward a broken bridge, it never felt like this. Like my brain turned to ice.

How could Virginia stoop so low? How could she insult me like this, so blatantly, and on Christmas Eve, too? It would have been so easy to make this delivery a heartwarming gesture, something that would have meant so much to me and to Ellis, but no. Heck, she hadn't bothered to drop the pears off herself; she'd sent this person to my door with a jumbo fruit pyramid and a bill for a hundred and seventy-two—

"Uh, miss?"

Brian the deliveryman was still standing on my porch, watching me with a little more curiosity than I was comfortable with. Realization struck me like a slow-moving slush ball —Brian was actually Brian Turner, who'd been in Melody's class back in high school. He'd grown a beard, but it was him, all right. His mother was Madge Turner, the biggest gossip at Holy Oak Baptist Church. Madge spent so much time peeping over other people's fences, she'd probably worn her own path through Sugarland's backyards. Stars. This awful turn of events would fuel Madge and the rumor mill straight past New Year's unless I could defuse the situation.

"The bill, Miss Long?" Brian prompted. "Would you like to pay with cash or check?"

Oh boy. I didn't have any checks. I'd been flat broke when my last checkbook had run out, and it hadn't seemed worth the effort to get more. And I hardly had any money on me tonight, only the remnants of the cash back I'd gotten last time at the grocery store, most of which had gone to buying Lucy a new bottle of Vita-Skunk supplement. Honestly, who carried a couple of hundred dollars around in their purse?

"Well, Brian," I began.

There was my emergency fund upstairs. My "worst case, do not break glass unless you're putting out a fire" stash of emergency money.

"I'll pay cash," I heard myself say, trying to sound perky and falling way flat. "Wait here a sec, please." I backed up and, once Lucy had followed me inside, shut the door on Brian and his fancy-schmancy fruit. I kicked off my heels and dashed across my freezing-cold floor and upstairs as fast as my strait-jacket of a skirt would allow.

I couldn't believe I was doing this. But I didn't have a choice.

I hurried down the hall and turned left into my grand-mother's old bedroom. Inside stood the big oak wardrobe in the corner that still smelled faintly of her lavender hand lotion, even after all this time. I opened it up and mechanically reached for the last hanger on the left, which held the ugliest coat in existence.

We'd been having a fairly mild winter, so I hadn't needed to wear my Technicolor dream coat much this season. The coat was a thrift store find, like most of my clothes these days. I'd been too poor for too long to give up my frugal habits, and given Virginia's idea of appropriate holiday gifting, that was turning out to be a good thing.

I pulled a slightly ragged letter-sized envelope out of the coat pocket and drew out three fifties, all that was in there. It wasn't enough, but if I combined it with what I had left in my purse…

Numb, I walked back downstairs and rummaged in my bag for my wallet. One twenty and enough change to make another buck fifty. I was fifty cents short. Heaven almighty. I could go out to my car and grab some change out of the ashtray, but then Brian would almost certainly report that to his mother, and—

Wait. Junk drawer. I needed to put the tape back anyway.

Two minutes later I had three dimes, three nickels and five hard-won pennies in my hand, along with the salvaged bits of my dignity.

I squared my shoulders, swept open the door like a true Southern belle, and handed the money over to Brian. I didn't care that his eyebrows rose as he jingled the change in his palm. Let him wonder; I'd paid for my delivery fair and square. "Merry Christmas," I said as I dredged up a smile for him.

"Merry Christmas to you, too," he said, scratching under the edge of his hat. "Do you, uh, want a hand getting this inside?" he asked, retrieving the fruit.

"I'm perfectly fine," I insisted, keeping my chin up, as he

awkwardly transferred the heavy, delicately stacked basket into my arms.

It was heavier than it looked.

Spine straight, I sashayed back into the house, immensely thankful I'd discarded those heels. Only once I was inside and alone did I let myself slump a little.

"How dare she?" I asked my skunk, who eyed my newly purchased fruit basket with glee. "If she thinks I'm going to bring this to the party, well, she can go…eat a pear!" I added as Lucy began dancing in place. Sure, she thought it was a grand idea. It was hard to insult a skunk.

"You want a pear?" I asked, balancing the fruit mountain against my hip. "You can have a pear. You and I are going to eat every single pear in this pyramid," I vowed, trying to keep a grip on the basket. "And we'll make ornaments out of the wrappings." If I had to take this absurdity on the chin, then I'd double down on it. Not a part of this crazy purchase would go to waste. I'd wear the basket itself as a hat if need be.

We hadn't taken two steps toward the kitchen when the doorbell rang once more. Sweet heaven. I changed direction and deposited the pear monstrosity onto the table by the door. Boy howdy, if this was a delivery from Virginia with a new bottle of perfume she expected me to wear this evening or a wardrobe change so I "appeared as though I belonged" better, I would…I would… I didn't know what I'd do, but it wouldn't be pretty.

I heaved open the door. "Ellis," I said on a sigh of relief.

My tall, broad-shouldered boyfriend looked amazing in a crisp dress shirt and tie, like a *GQ* version of the man I'd grown to love, but it was lost on me. I just wanted a do-over of the last five minutes.

His handsome features clouded, and his beaming smile transformed into a concerned frown. "What's wrong?" He glanced at the pyramid next to me. "Where on earth did you get those?"

"From your mother," I said, stepping aside so he could come in. "To replace those ham and cheese roll-ups you taste tested this afternoon."

"It's the pickles that make them great," Ellis said. He took a second look at the fruit basket. "My mother gave you a bunch of pears?"

I shook my head. "Not even close." I told him the story of his mother's surprise, the jarring price tag, and I finished by handing him the note. By the time he finished reading it, Ellis's jaw was almost on the floor.

"I can't believe she did that." He drew a hand through his cropped black hair. "I can't believe she wrote that. I'm so sorry, Verity."

"It's not your fault." It wasn't my fault, either. "It's hers."

"I know." He took my hands, raised them to his lips, and kissed them. "I'll pay you back for the pears and let Mom know that she's way out of line with this."

That was a start.

He wrapped an arm around me and rubbed my back. "Let's just relax and enjoy the party tonight."

"Like nothing happened," I said, my words sounding sharper than I'd intended. But darn it all. I understood Ellis wanted to have a nice evening with his family, but…

I drew back to look him square in the eye. "Are you truly suggesting we gloss over what she just did?"

His hand froze on my back. "No," he said slowly as if he were searching for the right answer.

I stepped out of his embrace. "You and I both know this isn't the first time." And it wouldn't be the last. "You've been calling her out for her behavior toward me since we first got together, and it hasn't changed her one iota."

Maybe Virginia Wydell thought she could commit any sin because neither Ellis nor I had ever truly stood up to her. Maybe it was because we always took the high road, because we approached her with kindness no matter how poorly she treated us.

Ellis cringed. "It takes time to wear down a mountain, Verity."

"There's always dynamite," I vowed.

"She's not the kind of woman who bends easily," he said at the same time.

"Ellis," I pressed.

"She never has been easy," he added, deflating. "It's not only you." He shook his head wearily. "The entire way over here, she was nitpicking about how hard I applied the brakes, how slowly I pressed the gas pedal. It's how she is."

"Wait." Reverse. "She's in your car right now?" He hadn't mentioned anything about that this afternoon.

He scrubbed a hand over his jaw. "In your driveway." He at least had the good sense not to bring her inside. "I said I'd give her a ride to the party since Dad is coming straight from the airport in Memphis." He reluctantly checked his watch. "And I'm sorry, but if we don't head out now, we're going to be late for the opening party toast. It's tradition. Montgomery serves his special recipe hot spiced cider, and he expects us to be there on time."

Montgomery would just have to keep it on the burner. "If Virginia can't make an effort tonight, of all nights, then it's proof that wearing her down isn't working. I mean, how long have I been trying to win her approval, and how much progress have I made? Let's see."

"Let's not," Ellis insisted, but I was on a roll.

"First she billed me for the entire cost of the wedding Beau and I almost had, and she didn't bat an eye when it looked like

I would lose my home to pay the debt." Ellis glanced out the window toward his car as I started counting off the insults on my fingers. "Then she went to my estate sale, bought the necklace my grandmother had worn on her wedding day, and made a point to wear it in front of me, flaunting it while she told me it wasn't up to her standards. Then she fed me pastries filled with rhubarb when she knows I'm allergic—" fortunately I hadn't eaten much, so I'd only ended up a little itchy "—and she faked having heart palpitations when we told her we were together. And she accused me of influencing your brother to quit his job as a lawyer in order to dabble in eclectic folk art, which is a career I don't think anybody even knew about until he invented it."

I was going to have to switch hands at this rate, and we still hadn't gotten to the way Virginia had of addressing me, no matter the occasion, like I was a particularly bothersome insect and all she wanted to do was swat me. Then there was how she treated Ellis.

"Verity—" he began, reaching for the doorknob.

"What about when she applied to Yale for you and said it was so you could finally do something worthwhile with your life?" I demanded. "Or when she said it was a shame you'd invested in a distillery instead of something 'upscale' like the Sugarland Express?" I paused to reel in my frustration. If I kept recounting Virginia's laundry list of offenses, we wouldn't only miss the Christmas party, we'd be here until New Year's.

Ellis pinched the space between his eyebrows for a moment. "I take your point, I do. Okay." He looked at me. "Let's start small. What should I do about the pears? How can I make this right?"

That was part of the problem—I didn't know how he, or we, or anyone could make this right. Virginia's snide, holierthan-thou attitude wasn't something that could be fixed in a day. I agreed with him on that. But the answer wasn't Ellis trying to fix it single-handedly, or me telling him how to do it either. Virginia saw Ellis's generosity of spirit solely as a weakness she could exploit. I wasn't like her. I wasn't going to take advantage of it.

"I don't have all the answers," I confessed. "I doubt there's a simple fix for any of it, but letting her get away with this isn't right." I gestured to the pears. "These are just the tip of the Christmas tree, and it's only going to keep growing if we don't take a stand. Don't you want to stop Virginia from torturing us? I mean, if you pay for these, do you really think your mother will ever pay you back, or will you be out the hundred and seventy-two dollars I scraped together just now?"

Hoooonk! A car horn blared from outside, and I realized it was Virginia, hurrying us along.

Well, she could wait until the rapture for all I cared.

Ellis glanced out the window. "Verity, I agree with you, I do," he said, digging a finger under his collar, loosening his tie. "But we won't fix an issue that's plagued me for my entire life in the space of a few minutes in your entry hall. This will still be a challenge for us to work on later, after Christmas."

"Sure it will," I shot back. After, later, tomorrow. Everything was always something to work on "later," but we had issues staring us in the face right now.

And I dared her to honk again.

We still hadn't talked about how Ellis really felt about my job, and piling his mother's attitude on top of that was too much "later" for me to handle.

"We'll take care of everything, I promise," Ellis vowed, reaching for my hand. His tie was askew, making him look more like himself than ever. "But right now all I want is to get my family together for the holidays and be a family, warts and all." *Hoooonk!* The horn blared across my front yard. "A real family Christmas feels harder and harder to pull off every year," Ellis managed over the blast, "and you're not helping by making us late."

I avoided his grasp. "Oh gracious, am I making us late?" Was I the one causing a problem? "Is the so-punctual-you-could-set-a-sundial-by-her Virginia Wydell going to miss five minutes of a Christmas party because of me and my pesky feelings?"

Ellis looked horrified.

Well, he should be.

"Verity, please—"

"No." Somebody needed to say it, and it might as well be me.

I hated to hurt him. I didn't want to make things worse, but I was tired of throwing myself into the line of fire again and again and expecting anything other than for it to hurt. I would not—could not—sit in a car with Virginia Wydell and pretend everything was fine.

"I'm drawing a line and it's right here," I said, pointing at the floor of my foyer. "And I'm going to tell her myself."

My discarded heels lay near the stairs and I fetched them, using the newel post as an anchor as I shoved them on my feet. "We're going to settle this once and for all."

"Verity—" He reached for me, but I'd learned to dodge from Lucy and evaded him easily. I swung the door open, heaved the basket into my arms, and went to tell Virginia Wydell exactly what I thought of her "gift."

3

I stepped out onto my porch to find Virginia eyeing me from the front passenger seat of Ellis's police cruiser. Her platinum blond hair, cut in a neat bob, looked as icy and unfeeling as her heart.

The pointed ends of my glittery heels began to crush my toes less than two steps down the front porch, but I didn't care. I was a woman on a mission.

My stride didn't waver so much as an inch as I stalked directly for her.

I balanced the fruit mountain on my hip like I was born to it and jerked her car door open. She startled at the gesture, or perhaps it was the sight of me advancing like a Christmas commando bent on making her wish she'd never picked a fight.

Virginia sat stiffly, almost too prim, in a tailored pair of white slacks and a red cashmere cardigan over a white silk blouse. She wore big diamond solitaire earrings and a matching diamond necklace that sparkled merrily in the glow of my Christmas lights. She arched a perfectly groomed brow at me. "Your place is in the back seat, dear," she said, her voice light but venomous.

"Not tonight." I was done taking a back seat to Virginia Wydell. "We're going to talk about the way you've been treating me and your son. Starting with this." I extended the basket toward her. My arms shook. I was so mad, and it was so heavy.

She peered at me like I was trying to hand her a dead animal. "I know your mother didn't teach you those manners," she said, slamming the car door closed. A moment later, the window rolled down. "How can you expect to fit in with that attitude?"

"This is exactly what I'm talking about." Her manner, her smugness. "Your intentions were cruel, and your gift—" The basket began sliding from my hands. "You can have your pears."

Virginia trilled a little laugh. "Oh no, Verity, I couldn't possibly show up at the party with something so gauche. A gift like that is appropriate for someone like you, but it would never do as my hostess gift." That was when I noticed the small gold-wrapped box with a red velvet ribbon sitting on her lap.

Ellis snaked up beside me. "Here, Verity," he said, trying to take my load of fruit before I dropped it all over the driveway.

But no, this wasn't for him. This was for her. "You," I said, slowly and clearly so there was no way she'd be able to mistake me, "behave like a truly terrible person. You're impossible to please, you hold everyone to a higher standard than God, much less yourself, could hope to reach, yet you have the nerve to act righteous while doing it." It felt like I'd uncorked a champagne bottle in my brain, and now that I'd started telling her what I really thought, I couldn't stop the words from spewing out.

"You say that everything you do is for your family, for your son," I said, jerking my head in the direction of a horrified Ellis. Well, let him see how to get the message across. "But, Virginia Wydell, in all the years I've known you, you've never put your family's needs above your own. Never! Not when Ellis wanted to become a cop, not when Beau was having trouble with work, and I don't know enough about Harrison to venture a guess, but seeing as he's never around—and I know you'd be flaunting him all over Sugarland if he were—I'm thinking he probably doesn't care for your company either!" Virginia gasped, but I pressed on, gamely keeping my grip on the basket though my arms were starting to ache.

"I've bent over backward trying to form even the most basic positive relationship with you, and you took that as a license to insult me, my family, my work, and now this, tonight." The fruit. The note. "I'm done. If putting up with you is the price of admission into Wydell family get-togethers, then I'm. Not. Interested."

Virginia appeared markedly paler than she'd started out. Her eyes were wider than I'd ever seen before in a non-life-threatening situation, and her lips were still parted from her gasp. I had well and truly stunned her.

Good.

Of course, it didn't last.

"Well," Virginia said, taking her time, drawing a weak, fluttering hand to her chest. "Are you going to hit me with a pear?"

It took me a moment to realize I'd reared back with the basket, as if I was about to dump them all in her lap.

It would serve her right.

I straightened. "I'm not going to get violent. But—" I'd meant what I said. "—I'm not getting in that car with you."

She blinked once. Twice. "I'm more than happy to spend

my Christmas Eve without you." Her lips quivered into a small but snide grin. "And here I was, thinking that you'd never find a gift I actually liked."

"Merry Christmas to you, then," I snapped. I turned around and almost ran right into Ellis.

He stared at me like he'd just witnessed a road wreck, but it didn't take more than a second for his natural chivalry to kick in. "Let me carry those for you, Verity," he said quietly, taking the pears from me. This time, I let him.

"Let's go inside," I told him.

Virginia wasn't getting another second of my attention or my company, and she certainly wasn't getting my pears.

I strode up the front porch steps, craving the shelter of home, needing to be back where I belonged. Where someone put me first, even if that someone happened to be a little skunk with a saucy attitude and a mild fruit addiction.

Sure enough, as soon as we stepped into the foyer, Lucy waddled straight for me, all nuzzles and kisses. "You're worth ten Virginia Wydells," I said, scooping her up and kissing her right on her cold little nose.

Ellis set the basket on the table by the door, then cleared his throat. I wasn't sure what he thought he was going to say. There was nothing *to* say.

"It's not that I don't think you're right," he began.

"I am right." We both knew it.

His shirt was hopelessly wrinkled, and his hair stuck up in places where he'd been running his hands through it. I reached up to at least straighten his tie.

He held up a hand. "I think..." he began. "It doesn't matter," he concluded, shaking his head.

"It does." His feelings counted. "You matter. We matter." He didn't have to look so miserable when I said it. He was letting his mother's smug attitude and false manners get into his head again. He was a good son, but he'd never satisfy her. "Stay with me tonight. Let Virginia walk to the party."

"Verity—" he began.

"Or drop your mom off, let her be with the Wydells, and you can come back and spend the evening with me." I was enough. *We* were enough. I touched his arm. "What have they ever given us other than hurt?"

"You make it sound so easy," he said, closing a hand over mine. He huffed out a chuckle. "You and me and no complications. We could feast on pear pie."

"My grandma had a killer recipe for pear pudding," I said, leaning into him.

"Poached pears, pear toast," Ellis said, warming to the idea. He drew me into a hug, careful not to squish Lucy. I breathed in the warm scent of his cologne and relished the feel of his arms around me. He was a good man.

"I wish this was easy," he mused.

"Me too." But he was worth fighting for.

His fingers trailed down my back. "I'd eat nothing but pears if it meant I could spend the evening with you." He tilted back to look at me. "But I have to go to Montgomery's house tonight."

"Have to or want to?" There was a difference.

"Have to," he said, without hesitation. Dang, I hated when he looked so earnest. "I have to fix this somehow. I just don't know how."

I drew back. I understood his point, but there were limits. "The person who broke it is the one who needs to fix it, Ellis. It's not ever going to get better until your mother decides she wants to change things, and I've come to realize she's never going to do that unless we force her hand."

He squeezed his eyes shut. "Maybe. I don't know. I do get why you don't want to spend another second with my mother, and I understand. Believe me," he added, when I started to tell him why. "But there's more to it for me. They're my family, and it's Christmas, and if I don't keep trying to hold them all together, no one will."

"Ellis—" It was a burden he shouldn't have to bear alone.

Shame on Virginia. Shame on her and her poisonous ways. She was mean. She was wrong. And somehow, she was out in the car listening to Christmas tunes while we cleaned up her mess.

"You could join me," Ellis suggested warily. "It's Christmas," he continued when I didn't say a word. "There's always hope, right?"

Maybe. I shook my head. "I don't know." I wasn't sure I had any hope left for that woman. "Ellis, I can't go tonight. Not after what happened outside."

I didn't regret a word I'd said, but I didn't exactly want to spend the evening with Virginia doing her level best to make me.

Ellis brushed a wisp of hair away from my eyes. "Family matters, Verity. And I hardly get to see most of the extended aunts and uncles more than once a year."

I knew the feeling. My family was the same way, only my father was long gone, and I wouldn't even get to see my mother this Christmas. She and my stepfather were in Durango, Colorado, riding the Polar Express while I took a trip on Virginia's crazy train.

Ellis dropped his hand. "I have to go," he said simply.

I didn't agree, but I didn't argue, either. He had to see this through and realize for himself there was no changing people.

I sighed.

What I did next I did for Ellis, and for me, and for everyone out in the world who couldn't see their parents this

Christmas. I leaned in and kissed his cheek, then his lips. "Go," I whispered. "Have a merry Christmas Eve."

He nodded and kissed me on the top of the head. "I'll see you tomorrow. Merry Christmas, Verity."

It didn't feel like one.

4

At least getting out of the dress was a relief.

It took some twisting to get my hands on the zipper in the back, but I managed to wriggle the thing off. I hung it in the wardrobe—right next to my now cash-free coat—and hoped to goodness I never had to put it on again. Melody could have her *CosmoGirl* style. It suited her. As for me? I slid into a pair of snowflake-patterned leggings and one of my favorite sweaters.

The gray-blue cable knit nearly reached my knees. I took my hair down and brushed it until it relaxed a little, then scrubbed off most of my makeup. I'd get the rest later.

I considered my dressed-down reflection in the bathroom mirror and sighed. How was it possible for me to be in love with such a wonderful man and still wish for a herd of reindeer to trample his mother? Or maybe for her to choke on a tiny candy cane?

Ellis and Virginia were so drastically different when it came to their temperaments and the way they treated people. I couldn't understand how anyone could act the way she did, I just couldn't. And it blew my mind how everyone had let her get away with it for so long.

Me included.

I fluffed my hair and headed downstairs. Perhaps I would make that pear pie.

After everything I'd said to Ellis tonight, every bridge I burned by standing up to Virginia and refusing to attend the party—I felt liberated, but also like I might have made an irrevocable mistake. I'd been looking forward to this party for weeks, and while I wasn't mad that Ellis had gone without me, I hadn't exactly planned to be alone on Christmas Eve.

Lucy waited for me at the bottom of the stairs, still eyeing the massive fruit basket.

"Merry Christmas to you, right?" I asked, heaving it off the hall table while she licked her little chops. "Well, come on, then," I said, hefting it toward the kitchen. "We have work to do."

I'd finally said everything I wanted to Virginia and put her in her place. After all this time. But now that the dust had settled, it didn't feel as satisfying as I'd imagined.

Be careful what you wish for.

My words hadn't seemed to make a dent. And now I didn't know if I'd ever be welcomed into the Wydell family. Virginia could now tell them—quite truthfully—that I'd dressed her down in my front driveway and threatened her with fruit.

Add that to the list of offenses.

Too bad being with my own family tonight wasn't an option, not with Mom still touring the country in her RV and Melody off at the bars with all her old friends who'd come back to town. Dad had been dead for years, and Frankie... well, I didn't know what sort of company he'd be at Christmas, but it didn't matter because I hadn't seen hide nor hair of him today.

I deposited the fruit basket on my kitchen table and tried not to laugh. It was kind of obnoxious. I'd seen these types of arrangements in magazines, but never in person.

"Time for a snack," I announced to my striped little sidekick.

She danced a circle and grunted merrily as I peeled the foil back from the ten-dollar treat. I'd done the math.

"We're in the wrong business," I said, handing a sliver over to Lucy. The pear was ripe and fresh. I'd just taken a slice for myself, the juice exploding in my mouth, when Frankie glided into the house through the side wall, right through the ceramic Santa in a sleigh that I'd perched in front of the parlor window.

Frankie always appeared in black and white, like a character out of an old movie, only transparent enough that I could still see through him. He wore a twenties-era pinstriped suit with cuffed trousers and a wide tie, and a fedora pulled low enough to cover the bullet hole a few inches above the bridge of his nose. You wouldn't know it was Christmas to look at him. Frankie didn't change much from season to season.

Frankie stopped short. "Nice look," he said, smirking at me. "Very classy."

I wiped the pear juice from my lower lip. "This is cute and comfortable." A combination I didn't take for granted, especially after tonight.

Frankie shot me a wry smirk. "I mean your sweater is on inside out."

Oh.

"I don't care," I said, resisting the urge to pop into the bathroom and fix it.

"Neither do I." The gangster shrugged. "You could be wearing a burlap sack for all it matters," he added, eyeing

Lucy, who curled around my legs, chewing her fruity gift with gusto. She didn't flee like she typically did when Frankie showed up. The lure of fresh pears was too strong for her to resist. "Anyway," Frankie said, halting on the other side of the kitchen island to stare at the pear sculpture, "it's a good thing you're here."

That was a welcome change from the way my day had been going.

He tugged on his shirt cuffs. "I need you to straighten out the lights on my shed. They're as crooked as a Chicago politician."

"Icicle lights aren't meant to hang perfectly symmetrical," I explained, going for another slice of pear.

"Molly's coming by in less than two hours, and I've got everything else perfect for her," he went on. Then he leaned in conspiratorially and said, "I made her an aspic salad."

"Aspic?" I racked my brain for a second, then clapped my hand over my mouth to keep from laughing. "Wait, you made her a *Jell-O salad* for Christmas?"

"It's fancy!" Frankie insisted. "It's that newfangled lime flavor, and it's got cream cheese and cherries and nuts in it—perfect for the holidays! I even made it in a mold! The thing's almost a foot tall." He looked so proud of himself, I didn't have the heart to tell him that Jell-O salads had gone out of vogue decades ago. What was a decade to Frankie, after all?

"Eh, what do you know?" Frankie said, waving off my amusement.

"She'll be here in around two hours, you said?" I asked, slowly cutting another piece of pear and chewing it like a sloth on vacation.

"More like one and a half! Come on, it's not like I can move 'em myself."

That was true. Frankie couldn't affect the regular world

other than manifesting the occasional cold spot. But he could lend me his power to interact with the other side, and that had been a game changer.

Frankie's power was the reason I became a ghost hunter. But it didn't mean I always enjoyed seeing *him*. I'd had my fill of difficult people tonight—dead or alive.

I put both elbows on the kitchen island and started nibbling on another pear slice. "I'll be out as soon as I'm done with this." It wouldn't do him any good for me to get it done faster. I knew my housemate well. He was fidgety already, and the longer he had to wait, the less time he'd have to think of other things I could do for him.

"Well, I don't want you to get sidetracked," Frankie stated as if I usually flitted from thought to thought like a butterfly in a field of flowers. "You're going to forget all about me when you see who's coming up to your back door."

"Who?" I asked, skirting past Lucy to take a peek out the back window. Maybe Ellis had returned to spend the evening with me. Most of the time, he parked out back if he was staying the night. Maybe he'd stood up to Virginia and wanted to tell me all about it.

But I didn't see him or any car.

I opened the back door, letting in a gust of cold air, and saw only my white wooden back porch, with its empty swing and the pair of silk poinsettias flanking the stairs.

"I don't see anyone." I didn't hear a thing, and Lucy wasn't acting like she'd noticed a soul.

"You will," Frankie said. A second later, he hit me with his power.

5

I gasped like I'd been drenched with a bucket of ice water. Everything tingled, including the roots of my hair and the tips of my fingernails. I swear, no matter how many times he zapped me, I still wasn't used to the feeling I got when Frankie shared his power.

"Gentler next time," I pleaded through clenched teeth.

"Whoops," Frankie said, with no real regret. But I forgot about him as a ghost began to take shape outside my door.

I recognized her immediately.

Donna had died in her sleep two years ago. I'd gone to her funeral. And now she stood on my back porch, appearing exactly as I remembered: messy gray braid falling halfway down her back, flannel shirt and corduroys, and a face so wrinkled that when she smiled, I could hardly see her eyes. Just looking at her warmed my heart.

"Verity Long." She broke into a broad, expectant smile while I stifled a gasp. "Oh, baby, I'm sorry to barge in from the dead and all, but it is so good to see you!"

"Stars." I could scarce believe my eyes. "You are welcome anytime," I managed, and I meant it with all my heart.

The woman who stood before me was a wonder. A lifesaver. Donna Lankin had changed my life for the better on a chilly Christmas Eve exactly three years ago tonight.

"You remember Lucy," I said, stepping aside as my skunk tore past me out of the kitchen and straight for the woman who had helped rescue her.

Donna had been on call at the animal rescue the night I found Lucy. December had been bitter cold that year, and I'd almost missed the little black and white puffball shivering in the sprinkle of snow gathered in a dip in the road leading up to my house.

When I stopped to take a closer look, I found Lucy, tiny and sick and all alone. She'd gazed up at me with those big black eyes, and I knew I had to do everything I could to help her—even though I'd had no idea what to do with a skunk, much less a baby. I pulled off my scarf and wrapped her up in the warm wool blend, then took her home and called the woman with the biggest heart in Sugarland.

Donna had been amazing, showering me with every bit of reassurance and competence I so desperately needed that night. She'd explained Lucy had been born in the fall—late for skunks—and most likely orphaned by a careless driver. She'd brought supplies for bottle feeding and a lot of practical advice on how to care for a skunk in my home.

Keeping Lucy had been the only option.

"It's not legal to keep skunks as pets in Tennessee," Donna had explained sadly, brushing a wisp of her long gray hair behind her ear, "but she's so young that if we nursed her back to health and then set her free again, she'd likely die anyway." At that point, I'd have cut my own arm off before giving up Lucy. Donna understood. She gave me the contact information of a sympathetic veterinarian who would treat her without reporting me, and she made plenty of follow-up visits to make sure Lucy and I were settling in well together.

"My, what a big girl," Donna gushed as Lucy ran right up to her and waddled in a happy circle around her intangible Wellies. "How's my girl, hmm? How's my sweet baby girl?" Donna cooed, bending over to get closer. "Oooh, I want to kiss your cute little nose, yes I do!"

Lucy grunted with pure joy. She shivered from the cold of the ghost, but she didn't let it stop her from getting close. Mind over matter, I supposed. Any actual touch between a living being and a spirit would deliver a chilling shock to both, but Lucy wasn't afraid to skirt the line. My skunk had always been a daredevil, and I think it was the first time in all her skunky life that she'd ever been fall-down happy to see a ghost.

Obviously, Donna had left an impression on her. Lord knows she'd left one on me. I'd never met anyone who bonded with animals like Donna, like they were instantly part of her family whether she spent a day or a year with them. She'd been as kind to me, too. I almost wished she'd stopped by before now.

"I see this little one remembers me just fine," Donna said. "You always were a smart one," she confided in Lucy before straightening up from her crouch with a chuckle. "What a lovely lady she's become. I can tell she's so happy here."

"We both are," I agreed, a little choked up. "She's a gift." We watched Lucy as she danced a circle around the ghost. She gave a wet shiver and a sneeze before gazing up adoringly at her rescuer. I knew how she felt. "I'm so glad to see you, Donna," I said, recovering. "Would you care to come inside?"

I didn't have any ghostly refreshments, but I could probably persuade Frankie to get something for her. I'd have to ask about keeping something on hand for ghostly guests.

"I'd love nothing better, Verity, but not tonight," Donna said, sticking with her spot on the porch. "I'm really not in Sugarland all that often," she said, as if embarrassed to admit leaving our small town. "I never thought I'd get around in the afterlife better than I did in real life, but it is rather fantastic. Not to mention"—she glanced down with a satisfied expression—"no more creaky knees!"

"That is a plus," I said with a laugh. Donna could teach a master class in looking on the bright side. She was the ray of sunshine I needed after what I'd been through tonight.

"Anyway, honey, I'm only in Sugarland today because I wanted to be here for my daughter's first Christmas with my new grandbaby, and as long as I was around, I thought I'd visit some of my old haunts—*ha*—and see if I could locate any animals in need of help. I've been at it all day," she confided. "That's why I'm a tad flimsy right now."

"Oh, you look great," I said automatically. Although now that I thought about it, she *was* more transparent than most of the ghosts I'd encountered. It seemed she'd been using a lot of energy lately.

Lucy returned to me, and I scooped her up and warmed her against my chest.

"I've already guided several of my former volunteers just a *teensy* way off of their paths to find animals in need," Donna explained. "In fact, I just helped Bree locate a nest of baby raccoons that were in danger of freezing to death over near Wilson's Creek. Poor things." She shook her head. "Too many folks driving too fast, and right through their habitats," she said, her eyes welling up a bit. "Their mama was never coming back. Just like with Miss Lucy here."

I held Lucy closer. "I'm so sorry," I said, wishing we had a hundred more people like Donna.

She wiped her eyes. "At least those babies will be looked after proper."

Lucy struggled against my embrace. "She has an independent streak," I explained, letting her down as Donna sniffled out a laugh.

"Just like you," she teased before gasping at my little skunk, who'd gone all out for Donna's attention by doing a handstand and waving her hind paws in the air. In any other skunk, it would be a threat display. For Lucy, it was the ultimate bid for affection. "Oh my, I wish I had a treat for you!"

"She's not short on treats," I said, thinking of the mound of pears waiting to be eaten inside.

"I don't doubt it," she said. "At any rate, honey, I don't mean to take up your Christmas Eve, but I need a favor."

"I knew it," Frankie said from the kitchen.

I hadn't even known he'd been listening.

"Anything for you," I told Donna.

I could practically hear Frankie slapping his forehead. Well, it was true. I owed Donna so much. And it wasn't as if I had anything else to do right now.

"I knew I could count on you," Donna said, reaching to clasp my hands before thinking better of it. "I've got one last rescue that needs to be done tonight, and I can't get any of my regular volunteers on it. The place is haunted, you see." She pursed her lips thoughtfully. "I didn't realize why this particular old mill gave me the willies when I was alive, but now that I'm dead, I get it. It's pure instinct for people to stay away from spots that are full of spirits."

Boy, did she have that right. Handling hauntings was part of my job, but not all ghosts were as friendly as Donna.

"The babies are trapped in the basement," Donna said, and

I can't get any of my usual helpers to set foot on the property. I've tried three times, and each time they turn back before they even get to the door. It's an...unusual haunting."

"Here we go," Frankie sniped from the kitchen.

I ignored him. "What's different?" I asked Donna.

She crossed her arms over her chest, and the lines around her mouth deepened. "The spirits are deeply rooted to the land. I felt it the minute I drew near. There's also a dark presence you'll want to watch. I can't put my finger on it. It was hiding from me, which is good. Maybe it will avoid you too."

"Doubtful," Frankie chimed in.

I wished he'd find something else to do.

"You'll be in and out," Donna continued, remaining positive despite Frankie's attitude. "It shouldn't be too hard. Not for someone like you."

"That's always the hope." It didn't usually turn out that way, but I shouldn't go in looking for trouble.

"Great. Now I'm stuck with two Pollyannas," Frankie snarked from the kitchen.

"Shouldn't you be checking on your Jell-O?" I called to him over my shoulder.

"I wouldn't ask," Donna said, "except it's a matter of life and death." She dropped her hands. "Verity, you're their best—and last—chance."

And I was honored to help. "Just tell me where I need to go."

Frankie shimmered into existence between us. "Nope." He held a hand out toward each of us as Lucy escaped to the kitchen. "Time for an intervention."

"Frankie—" I began.

"I let you yammer on. I let you have your girl talk. But I'm not going to watch your behind while you go do your do-gooding on Christmas Eve." He pointed a finger at me. "I have plans."

"And you," Frankie continued, turning his attention to my guest. "You said you'd stop singing show tunes—"

"That was the theme to *The Grinch*," Donna corrected. "I wouldn't necessarily call it a show tune."

"More like Frankie's theme song," I said to Donna.

Frankie turned up the volume. "You said you'd stop singing and get out of my shed if I let you say hello to Verity. You didn't say anything about haunted mills or skunk rescues or baby animals on Christmas Eve when I have my girlfriend coming over in exactly one hour and fifty-three minutes!"

Surely we had a little leeway. "I thought time didn't matter to ghosts."

"It does to Molly," Frankie shot back. "Especially when I said I'd meet her. I'm not going to stand up my girl for you or for anybody."

"If you leave now, you can make it back in time, easy," Donna said with the confidence born from years of experience.

Frankie snorted. "You don't get it. Ever since Verity made a deal with Ellis to clear out his poltergeist problem, nothing has been easy. Most of her 'simple' jobs take days, not hours, and threaten to stop my cold, dead, non-beating heart."

"Think of Lucy," I added, gesturing toward the skunk, who, from the sounds coming from my kitchen, seemed to be jumping up and down in a vain attempt to get to the pears on the counter. "Would you want someone to leave her out in the cold in order to entertain and eat Jell-O?"

Frankie rolled his eyes. My skunk had been treating him lower than a snake's belly in a wagon rut, and for some reason it struck a nerve. "I do like that little jerk." People, he'd stuff in a trunk. But I was glad to see he had a soft spot for animals, even one who avoided him. "Fine. We'll do it tomorrow."

"Now," I insisted. "These animals need to get someplace safe tonight." I paused. "What kind of animals?" Not that it mattered, but it would be nice to know.

"A sow and her young," Donna crooned, as if they were the cutest things ever.

"Aww," I gushed, imagining their little piggy noses and corkscrew tails.

Donna beamed. "They're the sweetest, snuggliest, little brown—"

"Absolutely not," Frankie broke in. "I don't care how cute, darling, blah, blah, blah they are. No four-legged anythings are keeping me from Christmas with my girl," he vowed, as if I'd asked him to burn down the shed rather than leave it for an hour.

"I'm absolutely going, and we need you along," I told him. "I don't know what we'll find at the old mill." Donna had warned that the ghosts were somehow rooted to the land. Ties like that might make them overprotective. And there was a dark presence. "We need your knowledge and experience."

Frankie had been a ghost for close to a century now, and he'd saved my hide more than once with his knowledge and instincts when it came to the ghostly realm. Not only that, his life in the mob had made him wary and observant by nature. I was too trusting, too open at times, which tended to either help break cases wide open or nearly get me killed. I was smart enough to know I needed the balance he offered. And the protection.

Even if I didn't always relish his company.

He gave a long sigh. "Just because you have too many do-gooder friends"—he drew the cigarette case out of his coat —"and you're bad at holding onto a man. And you can't put a sweater on right"—he slipped out a smoke—"and you ended up in solitary on Christmas Eve"—he tapped the end of the cigarette against the case—"it doesn't mean I'm available." He inserted the smoke into the corner of his mouth and lit a match. "I'm not on call twenty-four seven, you get me?" he asked, taking a few quick pulls.

"We still have an hour and a half before Molly arrives," I said. "Don't you think she'll be impressed to learn that you rescued a poor, defenseless animal on Christmas Eve? I know I would be."

He took a long drag and let the smoke escape out his nose. "You know what would impress Molly even more? If I was actually here for our date."

I planted my hands on my hips. "She'll be less than thrilled when I tell her you didn't want to help defenseless baby animals in danger."

Frankie glared at me. "You wouldn't."

Donna raised her hand. "I would."

Frankie dropped his cigarette. "Fine," he snapped. "But I'll have you know this is blackmail."

I doubted Frankie was exactly new to blackmail. "I'm glad you're coming," I told him. "And I promise I'll one hundred percent do everything I can to make this as fast as possible. I can drop your urn off here if we end up taking the mama and babies to a shelter or animal hospital. I'll toss it out the window if that's what we have to do to keep you on time."

"I'd like to toss you out a window," he groused, but he sighed when Donna and I kept smiling at him. "Fine. I guess, I suppose, I don't want to see any critter in trouble, even if all they do is tolerate me."

"There's that Christmas spirit," I said, winking at Donna, who looked ten kinds of relieved to have the help. I knew how she felt. "Let me grab a jacket and gloves, and we'll be on our way."

I cut a few more slices of pear for Lucy and fluffed her blanket before heading upstairs to the wardrobe. I pulled on the Technicolor dream coat, gloves, and after a moment's thought, the scarf I'd rescued Lucy in.

For luck. For love. And with the hope that we'd make everything right on this chilly Christmas Eve.

6

Folks could say what they wanted about my 1978 avocado-green beast of a Cadillac, with its purple velvet seats, monster front hood, and complete lack of Bluetooth. But one thing was for certain—it was reliable in any weather.

"Kind of fun how ghosts outnumber the living in my car," I said, by way of conversation as I cranked up "Jingle Bells" and steered down the long drive away from the house.

Donna smiled and gazed out the passenger-side window. "I love how you're starting the orchard again," she said, admiring the skinny young peach trees I'd planted this past spring.

"Step on it," Frankie groused from the back seat. "I think I could walk faster."

He didn't walk so much as glide, but now wasn't the time to point that out to him.

"It isn't far," Donna said. "Just left toward the river."

That made sense. There were a lot of old mills down that way.

We took Rural Route 4 South to the edge of town.

It was the way I would have gone tonight if I hadn't lost my temper.

If Virginia hadn't needed an overdue wake-up call.

I tightened my fingers on the wheel. At least some good had come of the confrontation tonight. Maybe I'd made Virginia think twice about how she treated people. And it had made me available for tonight's rescue.

"Now this way," Donna steered me down a windy stretch of road that was—again—all too familiar.

"Exactly where are we headed?" I asked, passing a farm stand that appeared the same as it had two years ago, crossing a wooden bridge that would lead us to a place I'd rather avoid.

"We're almost there," Donna assured me.

That wasn't my worry.

One of the things I loved about Sugarland was that you could get just about anywhere in fifteen minutes or less. The only catch was that every inch of the town came with its own history.

"Here." Donna pointed out a fork in the road I would have missed if I didn't know the area. But I did.

"I've been down this road before," I said, dread winding in my stomach as my headlights cut down a heavily wooded stretch of road near the river known as Kipson's Ferry.

With a sinking feeling, I recognized the creek that cut through the property and the start of the old apple orchard. We were drawing close—too close—to Montgomery's house and the party I'd skipped tonight. "This is Montgomery Wydell's property."

We were on his land.

These were his ghosts.

"I wanted to avoid the Wydells tonight," I said to myself.

"What's that?" Donna asked.

"Nothing." It wouldn't do any good to dwell on it.

I'd admired the trees slanting across the road when I'd driven this way with my ex-fiancé, Beau. Now those towering oaks made everything feel dark and desolate.

I began to sweat despite the chill of the ghosts.

"It's not far now," Donna assured me, pointing me toward a narrow break in the trees I might not have seen if she hadn't pointed it out. That direction would lead us straight toward...

I stopped the car, gripped the steering wheel hard, and looked at Donna. "Tell me we're not driving past Montgomery Wydell's *house*." Yes, we were on an important mission and, yes, I'd save the animals no matter what, but I'd really rather not take the land yacht on a cruise past the family homestead while Virginia toasted to life without me.

Why tonight of all nights?

And why did I have to drive an avocado-green Cadillac? There was no mistaking my car for anyone else's in town.

"I didn't see any houses down this way other than an abandoned shack near the old cider mill," Donna promised.

"This branch of the Wydell family used to brew cider," I said, cringing.

"Yes, the Wydells," Donna said cheerfully, "that's them."

Donna had predated my drama with Ellis and with Beau.

The light from the dash shone straight through her. "This is the most direct route and it takes us right through the orchard," she said. "The current owners largely ignore this part of the property, and nobody'll be out there this time of year."

"I really hope you're right," I managed. I believed in Donna, I did.

The car's shocks squeaked and groaned as we entered the orchard. It was dark, overgrown, and I had to slow down to a crawl to keep from bottoming out on the rough, rutted path.

But the rescue was this way, so we would go.

Barren apple trees stretched out before us in twisted rows, their thick, spreading branches black against the lighter sky. It had gotten cold quickly this evening. Mist crawled over the ground, obscuring the road and testing my headlights' usefulness.

"You feel that?" Frankie asked, sitting on the edge of the back seat as if it were made of glass. "The dominant ghost already knows we're here."

A prickle crept up the back of my neck. It did feel like we were being watched. "Hopefully they know we're here to help," I said, cringing as the skeletal tree branches whipped against the sides of my car.

"Don't be so sure," Donna said, watching out the window, as if she feared the ghosts of the old mill would appear among the scraggly trees. "Looks like there's at least one who doesn't want us anywhere near. We'll have to be fast."

"That is one area where you and I agree, sister," Frankie said, double-checking the revolver in his side holster.

The closer we drew to the abandoned cider mill, the more I could feel the heaviness in the air and the unspoken warning.

Get out.

"It's not too late to leave," Frankie reminded us.

I could see why Donna's volunteers turned back when they didn't even know why they'd felt the urge to drive down this road in the first place. Luckily for us, I knew the stakes. I'd help Donna and the animals trapped in this place.

Sccrunch! My undercarriage scraped something heavy and the car shuddered.

No matter. We'd survive and so would my car.

Ka-chunk! The Cadillac rolled over something tall enough to make it rock back and forth like I'd fitted it with hydraulics.

"Oh boy," I said as the bottom of my car caught on something. I took my foot off the gas. Whatever it was had stopped us cold. "What was that?"

"I think we're about as far as your car can take us, honey," Donna said, drawing her sweater tighter. "The path gets pretty overgrown from here on out. Don't worry," she added, ducking her head down through the bottom of my car and back up again. "Everything's still in one piece. You're just snagged going forward. You should be able to back out pretty easily."

"Unless we're stuck here," Frankie said ominously, eyeing a looming, moonlit hulk in the distance.

"You're not helping," I reminded him.

"The old Wydell cider mill is straight down this path," Donna said.

"Well, good." I killed the headlights, grabbed my purse and Frankie's urn, and got out, wrapping my arms around myself as I did. The chill of the night seeped through my Technicolor dream coat.

"You know, you could be at a party right now," Frankie said, gliding next to me as I navigated the large tangled roots twisting across the path.

"With Virginia Wydell? I wouldn't have survived the drive," I joked, dodging over a fallen tree limb. My tennis shoe slipped on something wet. Thank goodness I wasn't trying to do this in heels and a dress.

"My daughter should be opening presents right about now," Donna said wistfully, passing right through a gnarled trunk without noticing. "They bought way too much for the baby—he's only four months old. He doesn't need a giant teddy bear!" she clucked. "And Mary's husband is surprising her with a carved family tree he made himself. It's so lopsided it's wonderful. And then he went and made her my special chocolate crinkle cookies. She's going to cry, I know it. She's like me."

"You should be there," I told her. "We've got this."

"We do?" Frankie asked.

"Sure," I insisted. "Donna, you've shown us the way. You came to me because you knew you could count on me." I was certainly capable of rescuing a few little pigs. "Now please don't miss your grandson's first Christmas."

Donna looked to the looming mill, then back to me. "I'm sorry. When you're dead, getting there is no big deal. I didn't know we'd be hung up."

"Donna," I interrupted, "it's okay."

She chewed at her lip. "If you think you have it..."

"Trust your favorite volunteer," I teased. Then more seriously, I added, "I'll be fine."

"Hardly," Frankie cut in. "When Verity is tuned into my power—"

"No worries, Frank," I said, cutting him off.

Donna didn't need to know that I was as vulnerable to the ghostly side as any spirit when I held Frankie's power. In fact, it was worse for me because if a ghost was shot or injured, they'd heal in a matter of minutes or hours. If I was hurt on the ghostly plane, I had to deal with the real consequences.

"You said it yourself. It's a simple in and out," I assured her. "Go be a part of your family Christmas." It was the entire reason she'd returned to Sugarland.

She hesitated. "I mean, you should be fine," Donna conceded. "Stay off the upper floors of the mill where the wood has rotted through and you won't have any trouble. The animals are down in the cellar anyhow. That's where they used to store the barrels of fruit before pressing. It's a little tight down there, especially where they piled up some old pieces of the waterwheel, but I'm sure you'll manage."

"Go," I told her simply.

She gave a small smile. "I think I will." She hesitated. "Thank you, Verity. I don't think anyone could have handled this problem but you. You truly are a lifesaver."

I grinned despite Frankie's long groan. "I'm happy I can help."

She disappeared and left a frowning Frankie in her wake.

"Sure, you let her go to her thing, but not me," he groused. "Never me."

"You live here. She doesn't," I told him. "Besides, we can probably do it faster on our own."

"You really think that?" he asked as we took in the long, rectangular cider mill, at least what we could see of it through the fog.

Donna knew we could handle this. "She wouldn't have left if she thought it would be complicated."

He adjusted his Panama hat to cover the bullet hole in his forehead. "Lead the way, Kemosabe."

The mill sat on the edge of a cold, rushing creek. It was tall, at least three stories high. Pale moss clung to the rough-cut stones that made up the exterior walls. There were six windows on the side facing us, none of them still glazed. Thick, gnarled bundles of Virginia creeper wound in and around the broken glass like spiderwebs.

"Any sign of ghosts?" I asked, picking my way over the uneven ground.

"Yeah, they like to warn me before they pop up," Frankie said, gliding next to me.

I stopped short of the place. "I only hope the floor will hold me."

The upper window in the middle had a massive branch protruding from it, too thick to be an apple tree—it was most likely an oak, judging from the trunk I could see poking from the roof. The apple trees weren't out of the picture, though, growing so close to the building they almost seemed to be swarming it.

"Let's just get it over with," Frankie said.

"There," I said, pointing to a dark patch at the base of the wall. "That looks like a cellar entrance." And our best option. The front staircase had mostly collapsed, but the cellar stairs appeared to be constructed from the same stones that lined the creeks in the area.

And as I spoke, a guttural, droning growl filtered up through the cellar door, echoing off the stone.

"Have I told you how much I love going into haunted basements with you?" Frankie asked.

"Sometimes it works out," I reminded him.

He closed his eyes. "Why do I get myself into these things?"

The wooden cellar doors had collapsed inward, exposing a set of stone steps leading down into the darkness.

"Because we are needed," I said as I spied the shadow of a man in the first-floor window. A ghost.

Perhaps the very ghost who didn't want us on his property.

There was no going back now. And no telling what he'd do when he realized we weren't leaving.

"Merry Christmas to me," I whispered as I drew the flashlight out of my purse and descended into the ruined, collapsing cider mill.

7

I reached out to steady myself on the cold stone foundation as I worked my way down the stairs. *One, two, three…*

Dry leaves crunched under my feet.

I could do this.

A wispy cobweb clung to my scarf. With a shudder, I brushed it off.

The air smelled of mildew and earth and, faintly, of apples. Despite the leaves, the stone steps were slick with condensation. The walls as well. It was a relief to finally get to the bottom, on step thirteen.

"Molly is due at my place in an hour," Frankie said from a spot near my left shoulder.

We wouldn't leave his lady waiting. "We'll make it," I assured him.

The beam of my flashlight caught long wooden boards piled against the wall closest to us. "Those must be the pieces of the waterwheel Donna mentioned." My nose wrinkled at the smell of rotting wood.

Frankie let out a low whistle. "Forget about the cider, in a place like this they could've set up an applejack still, maybe two or three. Disguise them well enough and even the sharpest cop couldn't have nailed you without tasting it first."

"Your mind is a wonder," I said, turning my light in a slow semicircle in front of us.

"I really am kind of bummed prohibition ended," he admitted. "I now lack an outlet for my creativity."

Unfortunately for me, he'd found plenty. Like the racetrack he'd tried to start in my backyard this past summer. "I don't see any little pigs."

Perhaps it had been unwise to let Donna leave so quickly.

"Here, piggy, piggy, piggy," I murmured. "Heeeere, mama sow," I added. It would probably be an easier rescue if they were bunnies or birds, or even skunks. But I didn't want to discriminate. "It'll be fine," I promised myself as my light scanned the nooks and crannies.

The cellar walls were all the same dark, hard granite that lined the creek beds in town. It made sense. The mill had been built on a creek able to power the waterwheel. All the same, the rock didn't reflect light well. I had to squint to see across the twenty or so feet of cellar floor in front of us.

"I think there's another staircase across the way," I said. There was natural light over in that direction as well, filtering down through a big hole in the ceiling caused by the large, thick tree growing up out of the floor of the basement. *This* was the bottom of the oak tree, then.

"I think there's someone watching us," Frankie said under his breath.

"Ghostly?" I froze. Certainly not human. No one in their right mind would be down here this time of night—or at all. Well, except for me.

The beam of my light cut across the darkness, revealing

wet stone and broken casks. And then I heard it. A deep, rhythmic breathing coming from the corner near the stairs.

"There," I said, directing my light toward the crumbling steps. "I'll bet it's the animals."

"This is your show, not mine," Frankie said, letting me lead the way as we crept toward the noise.

I had to watch where I put my feet to keep from tripping on random chunks of wood, disintegrating cotton sacks with a stylized black *W* stamped on them, and the dozens of apples littering the floor in various states of decay. Some lay black and shriveled while others hardly showed a wrinkle. It seemed fresh fruit was still dropping from the apple trees invading the windows upstairs. It was kind of amazing that the oak tree was the *only* tree growing out of the floor.

"How about that?" Frankie pointed toward the far wall, where the hole in the ceiling joined with an opening that appeared deliberately crafted, most likely where the stairs originally started. Over the top of the hole hung a massive steel hook.

"What's that?" Thick rope attached the hook to a wooden pulley. The entire contraption dangled over the rounded edge of what appeared to be an old cider press. It all looked perfectly fine except...the pulley was spinning. Very, very slowly, but it was definitely spinning.

"Why is it—" As I watched, a thread from the rope holding the pulley in place broke. The pulley shivered and dropped a fraction of an inch downward, increasing its spin. "Oh, mother of pearl." The rope just a foot above the pulley was dangerously frayed.

The hook itself was big enough to impale something if it landed wrong. That, plus the pulley—they had to weigh hundreds of pounds. If they fell, they'd crush anything underneath. Not that I planned on getting anywhere near.

I shined my light into the darkness at the bottom of the ruined staircase, trying to make out the animals we'd come to rescue among all the broken barrels and sacks.

All I could see was an enormous lump in the middle of the pile of detritus, dusty and—furry? "I think we've found them." I took two steps closer, tiny ones, just to confirm in my head what my racing heart had already figured out.

Frankie stopped short next to me. "Is that what I think it is?"

I swallowed nervously. "It sure is," I said, barely finding my voice.

"A sow is a pig," Frankie said, as if he didn't want to be seeing what he was seeing. "A pig," he insisted.

"I know." He was right. Well, half-right. Trick was, a sow could also refer to a female bear and, "That's definitely a bear."

8

It wasn't just any bear, either—it was a mama black bear, with three little cubs nestled up against her rising and falling belly.

"Butter my biscuit." I backed away until my shoulders hit the far wall.

Frankie went right through it.

The large mud-spattered hulk of a black bear rolled to its side and let out a long, stuttering groan. The babies snuggled closer and I held my breath. I pressed a hand to my chest, where my heart thudded so hard I could feel it against my ribs.

That was a big bear. I mean, not huge as far as bears were concerned, but it could tear me apart like a chicken wing.

What had Donna been thinking?

She hadn't been thinking, that was what. Only two years dead and it had somehow slipped her mind that a bear could eat me for lunch. Or dinner. Or whenever it felt like a nice, juicy Verity snack.

I took a deep breath. Then another. *Calm down. The bears are asleep.*

That was a reassurance I'd never thought I'd have to give myself.

"Frankie," I hissed, spotting the tip of his hat through the wall next to me.

As if he had anything to worry about. A live bear couldn't attack the dead. "Get out here, you ninny."

His head jutted through the wall, up to his chin. "There's no need for name-calling."

"Or you hiding," I whispered as the rest of him stepped through.

"Force of habit," he said, straightening his tie.

And a perk of being dead. "I certainly wasn't expecting bears," I said, my breath barely a whisper. Or a mama one at that. "There's got to be a way to handle this."

"Like sneaking out the way we came," Frankie said, as if he were agreeing with me.

I gave him a long look.

"You are *not* going to wake up a bear," he said, pointing a finger at me. "If you get mauled to death, we could be stuck haunting this popsicle stand for decades."

His concern warmed my heart. "Of course I'm not going to wake a sleeping bear," I hissed. Hands on my hips, I surveyed the mess in front of us.

We did need to get mama and the babies out of the way of that heavy, dangling hook. Just because mama was dangerous didn't mean she or her snuggly little cubs deserved to die. And to be crushed to death? I wouldn't wish it on my worst enemy. And no question about it—that hook was coming down soon. I chewed my lip.

Frankie rubbed his eyes. "I told you this was going to take more than an hour. I told you we were in for a long night."

"I don't think we have that long," I said.

He jumped when another thread in the rope snapped, and

the pulley and hook dropped a little farther and picked up more spin.

For once, I hated being right.

Stars. It might be easier to move that pulley than to provoke a mama bear in her den.

Now that I thought about it, I realized that had to have been Donna's solution. After all, I was living. I could move things in the earthly realm.

There was only one problem.

"We need to get up to that pulley," I murmured. And the bears were lying around and somewhat *on* the staircase we needed to take.

I didn't need a lot of space, just enough staircase to tightrope one foot up after the other. I shined my light on it again and, well, that was a big bear.

"Don't even think about it," Frankie warned.

"I'm light." But with the three babies curled up next to their mama, there was no way I could get to the remnants of the stairs without stepping on someone. Even if I could make it past them, the stairs didn't appear too stable, especially toward the top. We didn't need a bunch of stone steps falling down on those babies any more than the pulley and hook.

"We'll find another way." I pushed off the wall. "Let's go back outside and slip in on the first floor."

"It would have made our lives a heck of a lot easier if your ghost buddy had told us to come packing for bear," Frankie said, gliding next to me, keeping an eye on the bears. I could see the glow of him off my left shoulder as I picked my way past fallen apples and debris.

Donna had tried to be clear. "We just didn't understand," I said, trying to escape as quickly as I could.

"I think she tricked us," Frankie insisted. "She thought nobody'd be crazy enough to do this if they knew."

"Don't always assume the worst." Donna cared about all living creatures, me included. At the same time, she'd been low on power and maybe she wasn't thinking straight.

Or maybe she'd seen an easy solution that I hadn't yet.

In either case, complaining wouldn't help. We needed to commit our energies to the task at hand, and I needed to focus on making it up the crumbling cellar stairs without tripping.

I took them deliberately—enduring the wet and the rot—and breathed a gigantic sigh of relief when we emerged into the night.

I bent over to regroup and enjoy the fresh air and the sweet, solid ground.

Safe.

Sort of.

But not done. I straightened and began searching for a nice opening to slip through.

There were three windows at the ground level on each side of the building. One of those had to be my ticket. I shined my flashlight along the wall to get a better look.

Dang. I hadn't counted on how densely the trees had grown in around the mill.

Twisted tree limbs blocked all three lower windows, and where there wasn't a branch there was leftover glass jutting from the window ledge. I'd navigated broken glass before when there'd been room to maneuver, but in this case, I simply wouldn't fit.

The front door appeared solid, locked to a stone frame on the right-hand side via an enormous rusted padlock with a long U-bend holding the two pieces together.

And that was it. No missing boards. No gaping holes.

"I think I need some lockpicking advice," I said to my ghost. It would be a dream come true for him. After all, how many times had he tried to "help" me break into places illegally?

I'd always refused.

But this was less of a breaking-and-entering situation and more of a rescue.

"In this case, the best way in is through," Frankie said. "That wood's gotta be as old as the mill itself. It's not going to hold up to more than one or two good kicks. Just give it the boot."

"And here I'd thought you'd want to show off your skills." I glanced down at my formerly white Keds, now streaked with mud and goo. They weren't the best shoes for kicking down doors, but he was right, the wood was completely rotten.

"I prefer a challenge," my ghost said. "A chance to be an artist."

Right. I leaned forward so I could brace against the sturdy stone wall, and kicked down right next to the iron latch beside the lock.

Nothing happened but the latch rattling a little.

"Seriously?" Frankie asked. "Are you trying out for the ballet, or trying to break down a door?"

I kicked harder. I was starting to get winded. Not that I'd admit it to him.

Luckily for me, he was nowhere near running out of motivational suggestions. "Come on, pretend it's one of Virginia's hoity-toity chaise lounges," he said as I shifted my purse around so that the urn banged against my back instead of my side, "or that gold-framed, fur-stole-wearing portrait of herself that she keeps over her own mantel, or her sinister, smirking—"

I lifted my foot again.

Crack! The wood around the latch splintered on the third

kick. I slipped sideways, but my tight grip on the wall saved me from a tumble.

"You see?" Frankie crowed as I stepped off the frame and heaved the broken door open. "You just needed to narrow down, tap that bad blood. You just had to think of her face."

I gasped and waved away the dust and dirt I'd stirred up. "I'm a nice person. I'm not—"

"You have a dark side, just like everybody else," he stated.

Before I could argue, a glowing light appeared in the doorway I'd recently liberated.

"Frankie, look!" I took one step back and then two as the figure lengthened into the shape of a man in a pressed white shirt turned up at the sleeves. He wore a tie and a vest with suit pants creased down the middle.

"Nice threads," Frankie said as more of the man began to take form.

"Can I help you?" the figure bit out, a little too sarcastic for my taste.

Then again, I did just kick down his door.

The man didn't have legs. Not yet anyway. I stared openly as his face took form. The squareness of his jaw, the dimple in his chin—those cheekbones. Oh, my word. He looked like he could be Ellis's brother. He had the same broad shoulders, same short, wavy hair, and the exact same eyes. In fact, he looked more like Ellis than Ellis's real brothers.

"I—" I gasped.

He studied me with the same exasperated expression Ellis would get before we'd ever dated, when he used to pull me over with his police cruiser and argue with me. This ghost was ticked.

I didn't know what to think. Except that we were on Ellis's family land, at an old family cider mill, and this had to be a relation, or my name wasn't Verity Long.

"Was that entirely necessary?" the ghost challenged, gesturing to the broken-down doorway.

"I'm so sorry," I said. "I didn't mean to cause damage."

"It wasn't an accident. You just kicked his door down," Frankie reminded me.

"Don't help me," I hissed over my shoulder at my ghost, who merely shrugged.

"You could have just knocked," the ghost said, which made him sound more like Ellis than ever. But paler, of course.

"We'd actually like to come inside," I said as brightly as I could. It never hurt to ask. "I'm Verity Long and this is my associate—"

"Rudolph Valentino," Frankie said without hesitating.

The 1920s movie star. The sheik. Sure.

"Never give your real name when breaking and entering," Frankie's voice sounded in my ear. "Why make it easier for this guy if he decides to get the cops involved?"

I thought we were done tangling with ghostly law enforcement after our last case.

The ghost looked at us like we were out of our minds. "Phineas Wydell," he said slowly, not making any move to invite us in. He probably knew Frankie was lying, and even if he didn't, we weren't making ourselves out to be very good visitors.

I grinned. "It's a pleasure to meet you, Mr. Wydell."

He waved me off. "Call me Phineas, please."

"Merry Christmas, Phineas," I said. "I'm sorry about the door. And"—I glanced at Frankie—"him." No sense sugar-coating it. "We're here to help some animals in the earthly realm. My boyfriend and I can come by and repair the door next week. But for tonight, I'd like to duck inside for a few minutes and move that big hook."

Phineas stared at me, but he didn't respond.

"Please," I asked.

He looked straight at me with those intense eyes, so much like Ellis's it was spooky. "If you want to step inside my mill, you'll have to do more than that."

"Here we go," Frankie groused. "Molly is going to be eating Jell-O alone."

"You'll make it back for her," I vowed. We wouldn't let this ghost hold us up.

Phineas's lip tipped up at the corner. "You've come here on Christmas Eve on a more important mission than you realize."

"I'm dead," Frankie muttered.

"Stop being dramatic," I urged, even if he was technically right.

The room beyond the smashed-in door began to glow with a soft golden light. It glinted off the dust motes and highlighted the broken remains of plaster clinging to the old stone walls.

Typically, the ghostly plane glowed silver, not gold. But I wasn't going to nitpick a long-lost Wydell relation.

"You're the dominant ghost, aren't you?" I asked Phineas, who merely nodded.

A dominant ghost controlled his or her location in the ghostly plane—how it appeared, what dwelled inside, and what could happen to me when I was tuned in. If the ghost meant me harm, I could be injured— or worse, killed by objects and events on the other side. I'd come close several times before, and it wasn't an experience I was keen to repeat. Despite how Ellis felt about my ghost hunting, I really wasn't the sort of girl to take unnecessary chances.

But Phineas seemed pleasant enough. He hadn't threatened me. Quite the opposite, actually. And after a little begging on my part, he was giving me what I'd asked for.

"It looks nice," I said to Frankie.

Phineas hadn't bothered to influence the gnarled windows outside or weed-strewn path leading to the place, but beyond the door, I saw gleaming hardwood floors lit by hanging lanterns.

"He's up to something," Frankie warned.

Of that I had no doubt. I'd be a fool not to think it—after the ghost's sudden change of tone, not to mention the way he was watching us.

"Come," Phineas coaxed. "Step past my threshold and you'll get what you need."

I didn't *need* anything. Except to move that hook and to keep the promise I'd made to my peevish ghost buddy.

"Err." I glanced back at Frankie, who stared daggers at me.

For once, Frankie was right. I had a feeling we were getting into more than we'd bargained for.

But I still had a job to do in that mill.

"Thank you for your hospitality," I said, stepping over the threshold I'd knocked to pieces only moments before.

As my sneakers crunched against the wood floor of the dark, dirty mill, I stepped into a completely different world. His world. It was still the mill, I could tell from the way it was laid out, but this looked…

It looked *amazing*. Laughing, chattering people lit up the space. Fresh white plaster walls reflected the light of dozens of tall candles. They glowed on every surface, including the enormous wooden cider presses. Garlands of fir and pine were tied together with ribbons and placed at the edges of tables and along the backs of ladderback chairs. A lantern hung from a familiar hook, only this hook was attached to a rope that was still sound. Right next to it stood a twenty-foot-tall Christmas tree, decorated with delicate glass balls and glittering tinsel. The entire place smelled of pine and the woods and dinner ready to be eaten. One of the presses was given over to food and drink, covered in platters and plates and, at one end, a gleaming punch bowl.

"See?" I turned to Frankie. "We're at a party! I told you it would work out."

"Give it a minute," the ghost muttered.

Most of the men wore double-breasted suits, although plenty of them had discarded their hats and jackets. Women in long dresses with simple floral prints punctuated the sea of suits like bright sprigs of mistletoe. The men shared friendly banter while the women, laughing and passing out food, occasionally called out to the children to "watch you don't get stepped on, Dottie! And, Ferdinand, get *off* the banister. You're not Tarzan, young man!"

One of the children ran toward us, and I instinctively drew back. Ghosts didn't like to touch me any more than I liked touching them, and I braced for the icy impact.

To my surprise, she went right through me without even glancing up. I didn't feel anything from it either.

"This is a vision of the past," Phineas said. A muscle in his jaw jumped, but then his expression softened as he gazed out at the scene. "The only actual ghost in here is me—and now the sheik," he said, indicating Frankie.

The gangster frowned, but I smiled.

"It's a beautiful memory," I told Phineas. "When was this?"

"Christmas Eve, 1930," he said. "I'm about to make the toast."

A younger Phineas climbed on top of an overturned crate. "Everyone!" he called. "It's time to taste the Christmas cask!"

Phineas cleared his throat.

"Is it hard to watch?" I asked.

"Yes. No." He never took his eyes off the happy family. "We used to wait all year for this. A celebration of everyone's hard work."

The adults whooped and clapped. The kids jumped up and down.

"I can see where you'd want to go back," I told him. I'd have enjoyed a large family like this.

"We loved this place." He gestured all around us at the shining apple presses and the spotless walls and the ornate brass *W* over the door behind us. "This was the first joint venture of the Wydell family. My father had always kept an orchard, but he'd never thought to do more with the apples than simply eat them.

"But my brothers and I, we knew it could be more. And once the hard times hit, it made sense for us to pool our resources." He smiled sidelong at me. "You could say we put all our apples in one basket."

He was almost as charming as Ellis. "I think that saying's actually about eggs," I said with a grin.

"Is it? Well then, we did that too. And it worked out pretty well. Kept the family together for years." He pointed at one of the ladies standing next to the apple press that held all the food. She had blond hair streaked with gray styled in a sleek, wavy bob. The woman was slender to the point of being wiry, and even though she appeared a little tired, she also seemed deeply satisfied as she handed out Christmas cookies in the shape of stars to the children.

One of the little ones clung to her leg, and she kissed the top of his head before lifting him into her arms with a laugh. "My father died the year before we got the cider mill up and running, and I think if we hadn't been around, my mother might have followed him," Phineas mused. "But she made it through that winter and then through twenty more after it."

The scene was so lovely, it hurt. "She clearly loves the kids," I managed.

"Yes, she did. No matter how many dishes got broken, or

how many frogs were hidden in the washroom sinks, that woman had the patience of a saint. The one she's holding is my brother Saxby's youngest." He gestured to the side of the Christmas tree, where a blond man who looked startlingly like Beau was standing, one arm around a pretty woman in a bright red polka-dot dress, the other gesturing to the man standing across from him.

"And there's my Charlotte," Phineas said, his voice full of pride. He'd turned his attention to a short blond woman busy unwrapping her contribution to the feast and already fending off eager fingers. "She's the best cook in the county," he continued, walking across the floor toward her. I followed gingerly. This place might appear like a dream, but I was still out of my element—and in an abandoned mill with at least one huge, extended hole in the floor.

"Hands off, you rascals, wait for me to cut it!" Charlotte was saying. One of the other ladies stepped in to run interference while Phineas's mother handed her daughter-in-law a long knife.

"I swear, I could try a dozen times over and my apple pandowdy still doesn't taste as good as yours," she said, bouncing the little boy on her hip. "I always remember the ginger and the cinnamon and the nutmeg...what am I missing, dear?"

"My secret ingredient?" Charlotte teased. "I don't like to brag about it, because it's hard to get in these times, but..." She leaned in close. "I've got an airtight store of cardamom pods at home," she murmured. "A smidgen of that ground in goes a long way."

"Cardamom!" Phineas's mother gasped and touched Charlotte's arm. "Heaven sakes, I never would have guessed."

"Nobody ever does, Mama," Charlotte said, and the women chuckled together as she began to cut the rustic-looking galette and lay slices down on plates. They vanished almost as soon as she set them out.

The air was full of cheer and laughter, of the genuine happiness of people who enjoyed each other's company. It was a scene that anyone would want to be a part of. "You are all so close." So loving.

"We are," Phineas said. "We were," he said, as if I had something to do with it. As if he knew what had happened tonight.

But that was impossible.

I shuffled a little closer to the ladies, wanting to get a better look at the apple pandowdy, to hear if Charlotte had any more wisdom to impart, to watch Phineas's mother cuddle the little boy in her arms like she never wanted to let him go.

"Be careful, Miss Long!"

All of a sudden the warm scene vanished, leaving darkness, cobwebs, and rotten apples in its wake. I reeled backward as I realized I was teetering on the crumbling edge of the chasm in the floor.

9

"Miss Long!" Phineas tried to grab me, which would have been shockingly cold and wet enough to make me lose my balance and fall straight down into that hole.

"I'm fine," I lied, stumbling backward, my gut lurching as my right leg slipped over the edge. Pain radiated up my leg, but I held on. "Oh, please," I whispered, my fingers catching on the uneven floorboards as I struggled up and away from the hole.

The fall would have been bad enough and—*deep breaths*—I absolutely refused to look down on the family of bears I'd almost landed on. My heart couldn't take it. The pulley creaked over my head, with its crushing steel hook waiting to drop.

"I should have ended the vision earlier," Phineas said, reaching for me again, frowning when I responded to his gentlemanly hand by scurrying away from him on all fours.

I stood quicker than I felt comfortable doing, considering the sharp pang in my knee. I was eager to show that I was all right. "It's fine," I insisted, making a cursory check of my aching body, all the while ignoring my pounding heart and the fact that I'd made a bloody hole in my new leggings. "I just got caught up in the people you showed me," I added, noting the room as it stood now, empty of souls except for Phineas and me. Frankie hadn't even bothered to stick around. "I had no idea the family used to be so close." And how they could fill up a room. It didn't feel the same in here without them. The silvery outlines of the cider mill mechanics stood still and lifeless.

Phineas cleared his throat. He looked to the place where his wife had stood serving apple pandowdy. "Most of the family has moved on, gone to the light. But I can't seem to let this place go"—he shook his head ruefully— "not yet at least." He smiled sadly. "We were very happy, for a very long time."

I was glad for him and happy to have seen a glimpse of his past, despite the...complication. But I was also curious. "Why did you show me?"

He looked down to the rotting floor, then back up at me. "It's important for you to know who we are. I know who *you* are, Verity Long."

"All right," I said, hoping he'd heard good things. I might have a shaky reputation among the living, but I'd done lots of good for the deceased in Sugarland. Still, I wasn't sure what I could do for him. The memory he'd shown me had been a happy one, and he obviously was able to revisit it any time he liked. "The Wydells I saw tonight in this cider mill were a lot closer than the family is today."

"We didn't have a choice. We were so deep in debt nobody else would have us," he joked before sobering. "It was scary at the time, but thinking back, it wasn't so bad. The lean times made us stronger, closer. And we did end up making it. After I died, my son, Phineas Jr., kept up the traditions as best he could, but..." Phineas shrugged. "After a while, it seemed that nothing could keep the family from drifting in different directions."

"It happens to a lot of good families," I said, thinking about my own. My dad, who was gone. My mom, who hadn't "had the time" to come back into town. And my sister, who was with her friends tonight, which was perfectly all right, except it would have been nice if we'd both had a family obligation instead. "I wish I could do something about it," I said, almost to myself.

"You can," Phineas said, surprising me. "You're doing something about it by being here tonight, by witnessing what I have to show you. What you choose to do with the information is up to you, of course, but I believe that there's a reason you came here tonight instead of the main house."

"It had more to do with a bear," I said, being honest, "not to mention this awful basket of pears."

But Phineas wouldn't be dissuaded. "You came to the one place where I have the strength to speak with you. That can't be a coincidence."

I preferred the pears and bears argument, but I wasn't going to debate it with him. Phineas Wydell seemed like a nice man with a touch of sadness to him. If reliving his past could make him a little less lonely here, then I was glad to have taken the time.

But as Frankie would remind me if he hadn't wandered off —I didn't have a lot of time to dawdle tonight.

"Well, it's been lovely visiting with you. But if you'll excuse me," I said, crossing over to a window, "I have a job to do in my own realm tonight."

Phineas watched, brow furrowed. "You're moving on," he stated flatly. "Are you truly thinking about what I showed you?"

"I'm thinking, all right," I said, searching the windows until

I found a good, solid tree branch that had broken from one of the main trunks. It was half dried out, the bark already crumbling from it. It was also freakishly long and mostly straight—perfect for the job I had in mind.

"Family is important," Phineas insisted.

"It is," I agreed, hefting the branch. I'd much rather be with my family tonight instead of planning how to stretch out over a crater in the floor so I could shove a pulley aside with a stick. "How did my life get so weird?" I asked nobody in particular as I drew as close to the hole as I dared. I gripped my stick in both hands, aimed for one of the rounded wood center pieces, and, "*Bam!*" I said, a little too early.

Turned out I was too short to reach over the hole.

Or maybe it was my stick.

"That's not going to work," Phineas observed.

"Thanks for the insight," I said, trying to keep the edge out of my voice as I started to sweat. I'd found the longest stick I could. What now? "Is there anything you can do to help?" I asked the ghost. "I just need to get that hook and pulley away from the hole."

The ghost frowned. "I wish, but I don't have the strength to move heavy objects like that, at least not in the mortal plane."

I nodded. Frankie couldn't either.

"We used to need a special ladder to reach that pulley," he added. "Once, my son George got a hold of it and—"

"Do you happen to have it still?" Not that I should be climbing on any centuries-old ladders. And I didn't even know where I'd place it with the hole in the floor.

"It rotted away before the floor did," Phineas said, deflating.

Of course it did.

Well, I still had my stick.

"Maybe I can make this work," I said, hefting the stick

again, thinking my way through the problem. So my stick was too short to reach the pulley. That was my first choice because there was more surface area to hit, but I could still try to move the dangling hook below it. I mean, the hook was thick iron. If I got it to swing away from the hole, the pulley was bound to follow. Maybe. Right? I hadn't quite made it past algebra to physics. "I can do this," I said, with the confidence of one who had no other alternatives.

"Here...we...go!" I strained over the hole—arms stretching, back aching—and poked the hulking iron hook with the very tip of my stick.

It didn't move.

Phineas eyed me skeptically. I adjusted my grip, choked up an extra inch, and tried again. This time, I reached farther, shoved harder, and hit the unyieldingly heavy chunk of iron dead-on.

It had the same effect as punching a stone wall.

"Bull's-eye!" I said as the hook barely moved.

No problem. I'd hit it again. And again. However many hits it took. And just as I was reaching out for another good smack, I saw in horror that my single, somewhat pathetic strike had caused the hook to begin another slow spin.

"Oh, that can't be good." I lowered my stick. The leaden, steady rotation did nothing to move the weight off its deadly path and—"Stop, stop, stop"—the motion began to fray the rope even more.

Stars. I turned to the ghost. "We need to do something!"

"We?" he asked, eyes widening. "What can *we* do?"

He might look like Ellis, but he sure didn't think like him.

"Frankie?" I implored. Wherever he'd gone, he needed to get back. Not that he could move anything, but maybe he'd have an idea. I'd just used up mine. "Frank?"

"I hate when you call me Frank." His voice sounded from the hole.

"Be careful," Phineas ordered, but I had already begun a quick scramble for the hole.

"What are you doing down there?" I asked the gangster, spying him in the cellar, crouching low over the sleeping hulk of a bear.

"I'm handling things," he said, and I could see in front of him one of the cubs was awake.

"Oh no," I gasped.

"Look at this," he said, making kissy noises to the little bear, who, unsteady on its four little paws, toddled toward the clearly insane ghost in front of it.

"Frankie!" I hissed. "We said *don't* wake the bears. You're waking a bear!"

"Just one," he said, tilting his head back up at me. "A real cute little fellow. And look. He likes me!"

He was out of his mind. "I don't care if a small animal likes you. It has a mother who will not." Frankie might not get torn apart by a rampaging animal, but I could.

He leveled a finger at me. "Somebody has to take charge of this crazy train, and so far, it hasn't been you." The little bear startled, and Frankie dropped back down and began tut-tutting at it. "Now I have a plan. A good one. I lead the cubs out one by one; then mama follows to see where they went."

Just the thought of it made me queasy. "Frankie, when a wild bear sees a threat—also known as me—it will not amble out the door the other way!"

"Like you're an expert on bears," Frankie said, as if he'd actually thought this through.

"The mama bear is right by the staircase that will lead straight up to a nice, juicy Verity snack." I wasn't sure what was left of it would hold her weight, but I didn't want to test the theory, either.

"You said this job would be no problem," he said, whipping off his hat and pointing it at me. "You said we'd be back in an hour." He stood, startling the baby bear, who ran straight for its mother.

It slammed into her side, making her grunt and waking yet another baby bear. "Frankie!" The second little bear yawned and then attacked his brother. "Get them under control," I ordered as the little bears began scuffling together, right next to the third baby, who wouldn't be asleep for long at this rate.

"It was under control until you started yelling at me," he shot back.

The baby bears frolicked directly under the heavy, dangling hook.

"That settles it," I said with a wince. It killed me to think it. To imagine it. To dream it. But I knew there was still one place, a house up the road, where I could find help. "I have to go," I said, turning toward the exit.

I'd just have to swallow my pride and show up at Montgomery Wydell's Christmas party in my torn leggings and muddy shoes. I'd face down Virginia Wydell and a dozen more like her if I must in order to get those animals to safety. Ellis should be able to move the pulley. He had a longer reach than me, and if my stick didn't pan out, he'd have his brothers to help.

"Hold tight," I said to Frankie as I headed for the front doorway I'd broken on our way in. I was nearly to the wide-open exit when the ghostly mill door slammed shut in my face. What the—? I gaped at it for a moment.

"I'm sorry." Phineas stood next to it, frowning. "I can't allow you to leave."

"I'm on my way to get help." In case he hadn't noticed.

Phineas stood his ground. "I didn't plan for it to happen this way, but you've given me no choice."

Holy Mary mother. "The last thing I need tonight is another opinionated Wydell telling me what I can and can't do," I said, reaching for the ghostly door.

The cold of it iced me to my bones, but I gripped the handle anyway and pulled.

It didn't budge.

"I locked it," Phineas said, with a cold smile I didn't like one bit.

I drew my hand back. "What is this?"

"You are here for a reason. A bigger job than you know," he said, looming over me. "If you go now, we will both be sorry."

I was already sorry.

And he was wrong. I didn't have to listen to this.

"Frankie," I called. I was done playing. "Cut my power." I no longer wanted to see Phineas or anything else to do with ghosts in the old mill. Once I was unhooked, I'd no longer be bound to the spirit realm, and I could walk out the door I no longer regretted breaking down.

"Just a second," Frankie said, sounding strained.

"Do it," I said, glaring at a smug-looking Phineas.

"I can't," Frankie's slightly panicked voice sounded from the hole. "He's blocking me. That's a jerk move, Phineas!"

So much for a friendly dominant ghost.

"You'd better not be hurting him," I said, my voice steely as I kept my eyes on Phineas.

"Your friend is fine," he insisted. "You are fine."

I'd be dandy once I was through with him and this mill. "You can't keep me here," I warned him.

"I don't see you leaving," Phineas said simply.

This was wrong. Out of line. "You are keeping me from doing my job," I gritted out. "And now you've trapped me in here with a nest of bears." Wild animals who would be crushed if I didn't help them, but who could kill me if something went wrong and I couldn't escape.

"I didn't want it to be this way," Phineas said, unmoved, "but you don't understand what I tried to show you."

"I get it." He didn't have to risk my life or the animals to shove it down my throat. "It's about family. You love your family."

"It's more than that." He ground his jaw tight. "There is another ghost here to see you. A stronger one than I."

"What if I don't want any part of this?" I asked, my attention focused past him and at my only exit. Locked. I hated to admit it, but Frankie had a point. Sometimes, this ghost-hunting business was just too much. "What if I just want to go home?"

"Oh, Miss Long," he said, his voice cold, his gaze downright chilling, "it's too late for that."

10

"I'm not playing," I said to Phineas as a second ghost began to form directly in front of me. Normally, I'd be glad to be the go-to girl for a ghost who needed to work through a few issues, but not right now and not when Phineas was being such a jerk about it. "I'm not talking to your new ghost." Unless it could move a pulley. "I'm not moving from this spot until you open that door," I said, seconds before the shimmering form of Vernon Hale appeared before me.

"Sweet baby Jesus," I murmured.

Ellis's uncle looked just like I'd last seen him, still in his police uniform, still strong and straight-backed for a man who'd been killed in the line of duty at sixty. I'd discovered him shot through the chest during my very first ghost-hunting case. He still had a little color—he hadn't been dead that long—but he'd faded more to gray since the last time I'd seen him.

"If you want to go, I'll get you out," he promised, hooking a thumb under his belt, his roughened voice sounding exactly as I remembered.

Stars. I still couldn't believe my eyes. "How are you, Vernon?" I hadn't had much chance to talk with him since Ellis and I had solved his murder.

He tipped his chin down, seeming to enjoy my concern. "I'm doing all right, Verity," he said with his slight Southern drawl. "Justice does that for a person."

"I'll tell Ellis I saw you," I assured him, thinking of how close the two had been.

Hale snorted. "Tell him I enjoyed watching him catch that fugitive in the alley last week." He grinned. "Aggie Foster should put his cell phone on silent before he commits robbery next time."

"It just cracks me up that Ellis had his phone number," I said.

"You know it's in the book," Hale answered.

As much as I enjoyed small-town small talk, I moved on to the task at hand. Hale was a problem solver, just like Ellis. "Look, I have to ask you a favor, and I'm hoping you can help."

"I've been watching. You want me to move the pulley," he said, hitching a thumb toward it. "We don't have much time, do we?"

"We don't," I said, eyeing the bears, as well as an entirely too satisfied-looking Phineas.

"I think I have the energy," Hale said. "But I won't know for sure until after I show you something." He exchanged a glance with Phineas. "A vision."

"Not you, too," I protested. "Can it wait?"

That way, Hale could rest up. Frankie could get to his date. And I could come back when it was light out, and when Ellis's mom wasn't right down the road.

"I'm sorry, honey," Officer Hale stated plainly. "It has to be tonight."

Of course it did.

"Right now, in fact," Hale added, glancing at Phineas, who nodded.

"The well-being of the entire Wydell family is at stake," the older ghost added.

"You realize I'm not a member of the Wydell family," I said, feeling the truth of that sting my heart.

"That doesn't mean you're not the best person for the task," Phineas said. "Please, Miss Long, all I ask is that you go with Vernon. See what he has to show you; then we'll turn our attention to the bears."

If I took too much time…if those babies died, it would be my fault.

The Wydells had been falling apart for years. How could anything I saw tonight help me fix that? But it was clear that I wasn't going to get anything done without Hale's help at least.

"Fine," I said to Ellis's uncle. "What do I need to see?"

Before I could blink, mist enveloped the space around us. I breathed shallowly, not trusting the air as the floor under my feet shifted and a new landscape took shape around Officer Hale and me.

We stood in a large comfortable sitting room with a fireplace crackling against one wall, the brass *W* from the mill sitting on the mantel above it, and a Christmas tree decorated with some familiar glass ornaments by the window.

"I recognize this place," I said.

"My in-laws' house," Hale said.

Montgomery Wydell's home to be exact. I scooted closer to Hale. "They can't see us, can they?"

"They cannot," Hale assured me.

There was Ellis in a very familiar suit, and there was Virginia with her scarlet sweater and the white pants she'd worn earlier—this was Montgomery's home *now,* tonight!

But this Christmas party was nothing like the one I'd witnessed at the cider mill.

There was no happy chatting or laughter. That was the first thing I noticed—the big sitting room was quiet, the loudest thing in it the crackling fire.

It wasn't that there weren't people in attendance, although not nearly as many as had celebrated in the mill. It was more that they'd chosen to withdraw from the main table, which was laden with enough cut turkey, collard greens, candied yams, and oyster dressing to serve a much larger crowd. It smelled heavenly, and I found myself wishing *I* could grab a plate.

The gorgeous banquet sat mostly untouched as the family withdrew into little pockets against the walls. After a moment, I realized why no one was congregating there. Virginia had staked her claim on a high-backed chair right beside the table and was upbraiding Ellis in a quiet but vehement voice in front of everyone.

"You should have stepped in," she said, her eyes narrow as she stared down her second son. "Instead you just allowed her to speak to me that way, your own mother! If I didn't know better, I'd swear you *wanted* her to shout at me."

"Mom, I don't tell Verity what to do," Ellis said with the weary air of a man who'd been repeating this ad nauseum. "Especially not when it comes to things between the two of you. But maybe I should have stepped in sooner," he added, "when I realized that you'd insulted her taste by saddling her with a huge expensive gift for somebody else."

"Taste?" Virginia sniffed scornfully. "What sense of *taste* do you think someone like Verity Long has? Is it tasteful to show up to a party with a platter of crudités that she probably picked up at a truck stop gas station? Is it tasteful to leap from one brother's bed to another like she's playing hopscotch? She was supposed to be your brother's, not yours."

"Mom—" Ellis warned.

"And now she's not good enough for either one of you," Virginia finished.

"I shouldn't have come," Ellis stated simply.

I'd wanted him to want to stay home with me tonight, but not because of this.

I felt utterly mortified hearing such venomous things come out of Virginia's mouth, but I wasn't alone. Montgomery's brother Owen, his bushy brows waggling, had started to make his way over to the pair but quickly retreated after hearing Virginia's tirade. In fact, several of the closest knots of other guests, most of them older, appeared deeply uncomfortable with what they were overhearing, shifting on their feet and murmuring to each other in hushed voices.

A white-haired man wearing a thick wool sweater sat leaning on his cane and leveled a snort in her general direction. "I worked the orchard for most of my life and was happy to do it," he said to another gentleman and a lady. "Wasn't 'til Monty's generation that things started gettin' *fancy*." He glanced not at Montgomery, who was talking quietly to an old man in a wheelchair I was pretty sure was his father, Phineas Jr., but at the third brother—Leland, Virginia's husband.

I'd only met Leland a few times before and had found him physically imposing but distant, even when he stood right in front of me. He'd always been too busy to participate in things like family dinners, holiday brunches, and birthday celebrations. I was kind of amazed that he'd deigned to attend the Christmas gathering, but even though he was there in body, he certainly wasn't there in spirit. He had his phone out and was scrolling through his messages, a deep frown on his face.

"Damn fools," he muttered before pressing a button and

lifting the phone to his ear. "Marjorie, get me Kline. No, I don't care that it's Christmas Eve!" he shouted into the phone. "Have you seen the load of documents coming in on the McDevitt case? If their lawyers aren't taking a break, then neither are ours." He walked into another room, still snapping out orders.

Out of the corner of my eye, I saw Beau watch his father leave, then upend a glass of champagne into his mouth, grab another one off the drinks table, and head for an abandoned loveseat by the glowing Christmas tree. He slouched onto it, took another long swig, and stared blankly up at the ceiling.

I didn't see Harrison at all. It seemed he and his wife hadn't even bothered to put in an appearance at the party.

"Well." The white-haired farmer slapped his leg and stumped over to Montgomery with the help of an aluminum cane. "Thank you for having us, but I think the missus and I will be going now," he said loudly.

Montgomery, who looked a little to me like a brown-haired Santa in a three-piece suit, wrung his hands unhappily. "Uncle Jimmy, are you sure? Susan's just about got together a round of hot toddies, and the Christmas cake is almost cool."

"It sounds delicious, Monty, but you know how it is when you get old. Your tolerance for these things starts to go down." I didn't miss the way Uncle Jimmy spared a glance in Virginia's direction. "Maybe we'll get together next week sometime, just the four of us, eh?" He reached down and shook Phineas Jr.'s hand. "Good to see you, Phin."

"You too, Jimmy. Bye now, Flora. Merry Christmas."

Uncle Jimmy leaving seemed like the start of a mass exodus. Everyone began talking about how late it was, how they didn't want to chance the roads getting icy, how they had things to do at home.

Montgomery sighed. "I'll go get your coats."

Montgomery's wife, Susan, appearing understated but pretty in a simple blue dress with a holly berry print, stood next to Phineas Jr.'s chair, holding a tray of steaming cider-scented toddies in her hands. Tears stood out in her big brown eyes. "No," she said to her husband. "I looked up a bunch of classic cider drink recipes. Hot apple cider buttered rum, apple pie sparklers, pumpkin-cider fizz. And I made them all. Not that anyone has to try them all, but surely it's too soon for everyone to leave."

Phineas Jr. reached up and patted her arm. "I'm sorry about that, my dear," he said, and I heard remnants of his father in his kind but firm tones. "But it'll take more than cocktails to mellow this crowd. I think this might be the last Wydell family Christmas party. It seems like an awful lot of trouble to go to these days when so many people seem unable to enjoy it."

"But...but...I have a surprise," Susan announced, appearing flustered, as if she couldn't quite believe she'd just said that. "Stay," she urged Uncle Jimmy and his crowd. "It won't take long, and it would mean the world to me."

Jimmy hesitated for a moment before giving a quick nod. "Sure, Susan. I'm sorry. We'd be glad to stay a little longer if it would make you happy."

She and Montgomery helped them find new seats by the fire. It was clear Susan had tried her best, but there was no telling how long she'd be able to keep everyone together.

And I certainly didn't think drinking was the answer.

Ellis, who'd finally escaped from Virginia's clutches, wandered over to sit next to Beau. He glanced at his brother like he wanted to say something to him, but after a few moments, he sighed and looked away instead.

Virginia strolled over to take a hot toddy off Susan's tray. "Perhaps more people would be eager to stay," she said cuttingly, "if the food was better. I told you to hire my caterer."

Susan bit her lip, set the tray down on the nearest table, and walked quickly back into the kitchen.

Behind her, Aunt Flora stood staring with her coat half-on, as shocked as if someone had slapped her.

Uncle Jimmy slid the coat the rest of the way up her shoulders. "Yep. I definitely feel my arthritis coming on. Must be the chill in the air. Best get home."

"Oh my God." I pressed my hands to my hot cheeks, feeling a wave of secondhand embarrassment flood my whole body. "She's out of control."

Officer Hale nodded grimly. "My sister Virginia has never been the kindest soul, but she came here tonight raring to pick a fight."

"Because I told her off earlier," I said.

Officer Hale sighed.

"She deserved it," I told him. "In fact, she deserves it again right now."

"That might be true, Verity. But some parts of this family have been broken for a long time." He wasn't looking at Virginia. He was staring at his nephews, side by side but totally alone for all they were connecting with each other. "It doesn't help that my brother-in-law is a damn fool who thinks money is the most important thing in life, never mind how his boys have suffered without him."

"Phineas wants me to do something about this, but…" I gestured helplessly around the room. "What could I possibly do to make a difference, when people who are actually part of the family can't?" It was clear that Montgomery and his wife were trying, but they were fighting against forces that were bigger than themselves. Time was slowly but surely taking away the Wydells who remembered how Christmas as a family used to be, and too few people in the later generations seemed to care about the old traditions.

"I don't know what you can do," Officer Hale confessed. "Hell, I don't know what *I* could have done back when I was alive, other than grab my sister by the scruff of her neck and haul her out back for a good talking-to. The Wydells welcomed us into their family, and she brought them nothing but trouble."

"No wonder Ellis needed you," I said.

His uncle had been his mentor and friend, the reason he'd joined the police force.

"I tried to be a good influence on the kids, but now I think I should have stuck my nose in more. Look at my nephews. They need the support of their family more than ever, and I'm helpless to do anything about it. I hate it." He shook his head. "I should have tried harder when I had the chance. I wish to God I had."

We stood in silence for a long moment before the scene began to fade away, the nearly empty room vanishing in a whirl of white.

11

Returning to the cider mill was less of a rude awakening this time, almost a relief. My stomach churned with the thought of what I'd just seen. "Phineas." I turned to search for the ghost who was the architect of my journey. He stood a few feet behind me, his handsome face solemn, his mouth turned down at the corners.

"Miss Long." He inclined his head. "Welcome back."

I was done with niceties. "Why are you showing me this? There's nothing I can do." There was nothing Hale could do. It wasn't nice or fair, but it was fact.

"You needed to see," Phineas said, as if that was all there was to it.

That didn't help at all.

I didn't create this. I didn't make Virginia into the person she'd become. And it was abundantly clear that I couldn't fix it. "I already tried putting my foot down on Virginia's bad behavior once tonight, and all it got me was excluded."

Although from what I'd seen tonight, that was a good thing.

Phineas exchanged a look with Hale, who scrubbed a hand over his jaw. "Verity," Hale said pragmatically, "the stand you took tonight was what drew you to this place."

Hardly. "I think my friend did that."

And speaking of such…

I peeked over the edge of the hole in the floor and saw Frankie tossing ghostly apples at the sleeping bear—over her massive front paws, *through* her head—to the delight of all three babies, who danced all around her massive slumbering form like this was some kind of game. "Chase!" Frankie called to them. "Go!"

Oh, sweet baby Jesus. "Frankie!" I whispered as loudly as I could. This was too much. Too far. Frankie might not get torn apart by a rampaging animal, but I could. "What happened to leading the babies out?"

He stood in the hole, looking like a slightly overwhelmed babysitter. "They won't leave. They won't chase apples," he said, tossing his hands up. "They're completely out of control!"

"They're going to get me mauled!"

"Don't be dramatic," the ghost said, wincing as a baby climbed its sleeping mother's snout. "Okay, that was bad," he admitted. He pointed to the bear. "That's enough out of you, Sprinkles."

"Sprinkles?"

"He's got gray dots on his nose," Frankie said fondly before catching himself. "Look, that pulley is falling soon, and these little guys need to skedaddle."

"My point exactly." If he'd only listen to reason, at least attempt to be a responsible adult.

He dropped his remaining apple. "At least I'm doing something. You're too busy taking ghost taxis to remember the actual reason we're here."

"I'm working on it," I said, catching sight of Phineas by the door. "You said I could go after I went with Hale."

"I made no such promise," Phineas said.

"You haven't truly grasped the lesson yet," Hale added.

"Now you're in on it too?" I asked the former officer. For the love of Pete. "I know enough." We were running out of time.

Hale's mouth formed a thin line, but I saw him blink.

"I listened to you," I said. "Now you help me. We need to get that pulley moved before it falls."

Hale gave a sharp nod. "You're right. Let's try. It's a hell of a big piece of machinery." He studied the problem for a moment. "Let's do it this way: I'll swing it toward you, and when it's close enough, you can grab the hook and pull it over the rest of the way."

And hope it didn't break off and fall on me.

I really didn't like the idea of intercepting a massive, heavy hook, but it was worth a try. "It's a plan."

"My plan's better," Frankie said from the hole.

We both ignored him.

"All right, then." Officer Hale floated just behind the pulley, his jaw clenched like a boxer entering the ring. He took a few deep, fast breaths—mentally psyching himself up, I figured, since it wasn't as if he needed the air—and then began to push. His form began to blur, the clean edges of his spectral body melding and clustering together until he was just a ball of light centered right behind the pulley.

It didn't move.

"Push harder," I urged, bracing against the intensifying chill. My breath frosted the air in front of me.

The ball of light quivered.

"Yes!" I said as the layer of dust covering the hook exploded off it in a thick gray cloud.

But the pulley itself didn't shift even an inch.

Oh no. "Maybe try a different angle," I suggested.

The image of Officer Hale reformed, this time barely visible. His head was completely transparent, the rest of him a mist. He gasped and glared at the pulley. "It's too much," he said, shaking his head. "I used up my juice. I can't get it to you, Verity."

"I appreciate you trying," I said. What he'd done to himself couldn't have been comfortable. "Now you have to get me out of here."

"We have a bigger problem," Officer Hale said tentatively. I wasn't used to tentative from him. He was forthright, determined, never one to hesitate. He glanced at Phineas. "She's here?"

And as he said it, the air in the mill grew even colder.

"I'd been hoping to avoid this," Phineas said, stiffening. The boards of the old mill began to creak and shudder.

"Who is it?" I asked, bracing for who knew what.

"A strong spirit. One of the strongest I've ever met," Hale said. "She's tied to the land."

"And she's lingering just outside the door," Phineas added.

Donna had warned me about a dark presence. It seemed I was about to meet her.

Phineas exchanged a wary glance with Hale. "I was afraid this would happen if you or I didn't succeed."

"Me too." Hale dug his hands into his pockets. "But it's worth a shot."

No, it wasn't. "We don't have to do this," I said.

"I could allow her inside just this once," Phineas ventured. "In truth, the boundary that I've set is more of a formality for her than a rule. She is"—he shuddered slightly— "quite powerful."

Powerful enough to scare Donna. Threatening enough to

give any living person pause. And with Frankie's power, I was vulnerable on every level.

"Uh, Verity…" Frankie called. "Why's it getting dark down here?"

"Hang tight, Frank."

Powerful might mean that the ghost could help us move the pulley, but it could just as easily mean she'd have no interest in helping. Almost all the ghosts I'd met before who had the ability to affect the physical world had been, well… It would be generous to call them "emotionally unstable."

Hale's image flickered. "For what it's worth, I don't think she wants to hurt you," he said. "But she wouldn't be here if she didn't have something to show you. Something bleak."

I stared at him uncertainly. "Worse than what you already showed me?" I didn't know how it could get much worse.

"Dark but necessary," Phineas insisted. That guy was really starting to get on my nerves.

The wrecking ball of a hook jerked into a fresh rotation as another strand of rope directly above it snapped. Then another. I watched in horror as it dropped farther away from the pulley, a fraction of an inch closer to disaster.

"Verity," Frankie shouted, "you've got to hurry."

The rope wasn't going to last much longer—maybe not even as long as it would take me to get to the main house and back, assuming I could convince Phineas to let me go this time.

I can do this.

One more journey with one more ghost—one that might or might not help me after.

No. I'd convince her. I would. I braced myself. "I'll go."

Phineas nodded and closed his eyes. A moment later a fresh chill came over me—not the same as the chill I was standing in, but a cold that came from a dark night, winter winds, and a dusting of snow on the ground. This was the chill of the grave, an icy blast from the beyond that felt like it reached inside me and froze my soul. I bent almost double as the harshness of it racked me then gradually receded like a malevolent tide.

"Be cautious with her!" I heard Phineas shout. "The living are fragile!"

"Too fragile," the new ghost agreed. Her voice was low and crackly, like breaking ice. I caught my breath and straightened to greet her, but as soon as I saw her, my own voice evaporated.

She was like no ghost I'd ever seen before. She floated before me, wreathed in a flowing gray cloak pulled close around her figure. I tried to make out her face. At least, where her face *should* be. The oval within the hood of the cloak was nothing but a swirling black hole that swallowed the light from the room. "Verity Long," the spirit intoned, "you have a task to complete." A bony finger beckoned me. "This way."

I didn't want to go, not with her. But the rope was fraying before my eyes.

"I'll go," I said quickly, "but I need you to do a quick favor for me first." I made it a statement, as if it were a done deal. "You need to move that pulley away from the hole. There isn't much time left."

"The journey shall take no physical time at all," the ghost said. "But it will exact a toll."

I didn't want any more tolls or journeys or ghosts tonight. "Do we have a deal?" I pressed.

"After," the ghost answered. "Once you learn."

The only thing I'd learned tonight was that Wydells—and their ghosts—were a pain in my rear. But we didn't have time to argue, and it was probably as good a deal as I was going to get. "All right. Fine. Let's do this."

"Good luck," Hale's voice sounded in my ear.

When I'd traveled with Phineas, stepping into another time had been as simple as walking through a door. With Officer Hale, the cider mill had faded into Montgomery Wydell's house in a flurry of mist.

When the power of this ghost swirled around me, it felt like being plunged into a pool of icy water. The room faded, the light vanished, and my lungs squeezed tight in my chest. I couldn't think. I couldn't breathe. I struggled against the pain and the void until bright white light made me slam my eyes closed.

I choked out a breath, shielding my face against the glare. "What is this place?"

"The future is never easy to look upon," the ghost's voice crackled.

"The future?" That got my attention. I blinked and realized I was in a small room with piano music playing.

Only I didn't see a piano. Just beige walls, a neatly made beige medical bed, and Virginia Wydell sitting in a straight-back chair, wearing pearl earrings and a red silk housecoat, and looking about a century old.

Her silver hair had been styled in the same familiar bob. And she directed an equally familiar icy glare at a nurse in holly berry scrubs.

"How dare you bring that monstrosity into my room," Virginia demanded, pointing at a foot-tall foil Christmas tree with red plastic balls on the end of each bough. "It's not mine."

The kind-eyed nurse folded her hands in front of her. "Well, Mrs. Wydell, I thought it might brighten up your day. Mr. Flatley in 204 is out with his family until after the holiday, so he won't miss it."

"It's pathetic and so is he," Virginia spat. But I noticed she had no decorations, no family notes or mementos. No old photographs in her room. Only expensive, sterile decorations —a crystal vase with dried-up flowers, painted nature scenes in frames.

"I'm sorry you feel that way," the nurse said, her tone hardening as she removed the tree and walked out the door.

"No wonder nobody visits that one," said another nurse passing by.

"I feel sorry for her," said the nurse with the tree. "Nobody talks to her. Nobody visits."

"Close the door!" Virginia demanded.

"Sure, dear." The institutional door snicked shut, and Virginia sat alone. She stared out the window at the parking lot, a bitter frown creasing her sunken lips.

It was a sad and depressing scene, but it also felt warm and right as I saw what she'd become, a shrunken shell of toxic pride that had left her completely alone. Good.

Justice had been served.

The laughter bubbled up, and even though I wasn't rude enough to let it out, it felt so wonderful inside my own head. She'd made her bed, and I was deeply glad she was wallowing in it. "It's what she deserves," I said to the ghost.

And as I said it out loud, I paused.

That wasn't me. I'd never been the kind of person to take joy in someone else's suffering.

Virginia Wydell was the most poisonous person I'd ever met, and I didn't know how many times I'd wished others would realize what I had. Life was too short to put up with her brand of venom.

But if I let her make me into a person who took joy in another person's misery—even Virginia Wydell's—then she would win no matter what happened.

The ghost bowed her head, looking away from what Virginia had become. "Have you seen enough?" she asked me.

"I have," I said, watching a defiant Virginia stare out the window as cars pulled in and out of the lot.

Virginia's venom had been neutralized at last.

The mist of the ghost swirled around me, blotting out Virginia and the pain she'd caused—to herself this time.

I braced against the ice and the pressure and held my breath as the world spun around me. When at last it felt safe to remove my hands from my eyes and open them, I stood gasping in a field under the light of the moon.

"Are we back?" I asked. I'd expected the old cider mill.

My gaze caught the stars, then traveled downward.

The ghost hadn't returned me to the mill or Montgomery's warm if dysfunctional house. Instead we stood outside on a leaf-strewn path. Then in the dim light I made out rows of shadowy gravestones. "This is a cemetery."

The ghost didn't say anything.

"Why aren't we back at the mill?" I didn't understand.

Her voice crackled over me. "You still have to see."

I'd seen plenty. More than enough, in fact. "Is this the same Christmas Eve you showed me before?"

"It is," the ghost murmured.

I recognized this place. And it wouldn't have been my first choice for a holiday visit.

Holy Oak Cemetery stood about a mile away from Ellis's brewery, on the south side of town. There was a newer one closer to Sugarland's town center, but sometimes people with long family histories in town were still interred out here. Maybe Virginia had died. No, I'd just seen her.

The sound of footsteps made me turn in time to see a very familiar man carrying a single white stargazer lily. My blood froze in my veins. "Ellis."

The beam of his flashlight cut through the dark night, and

he stared straight ahead with no emotion as he walked straight through me.

"Ellis!" I hurried after him, not caring if the ghost followed or left me. Ellis looked terrible, hollowed out through his cheeks and temples like he'd lost ten pounds too fast. The circles under his eyes were dark enough for me to see despite the low light, and his walk was more like a trudge, every step an effort he almost couldn't seem to bear.

The worst of it was the expression he wore, like his heart had been ripped out.

I caught up to him. "I'm here." He was miserable and hurting, and I couldn't keep myself from reaching a hand out toward him. I would do anything to take that awful look off his face.

But my hand passed straight through him.

"I should be here with him," I said as he continued down the leafy path without me, away from the main cemetery and into the woods. The ghost drew up next to me. "Why am I not here with him?" I asked. "If this is Christmas Eve, then we should be together." Especially if the alternative was him walking through a graveyard all by himself.

The ghost made no move to speak. She just watched.

I mean, if what I'd seen at the nursing home were true, Virginia Wydell was no longer able to make us miserable and mess with our lives.

This should be a happy time.

"Your heart hardened," the ghost said simply.

"I grew a spine," I said. "And I was right." I didn't regret standing up to Virginia, not one bit.

But at the same time, an uncomfortable realization settled over me. Seeing her just now, alone and abandoned in that home, I'd been happy.

If it had been someone else—anyone else—I'd have at least felt sorry for them.

But surely it was a small thing, and I'd caught myself.

There were more important matters to worry about.

"What happened to Ellis and me?" The possibility that I wouldn't be there at his side, that I wasn't a part of his life, astounded me.

The ghost's tone darkened. "You changed."

I couldn't have changed that much. I never imagined the future wouldn't turn out with us together. I'd never thought that there was anything the two of us couldn't handle. But even if I'd been left with a broken heart, even if we weren't meant to be, I wanted the best for him. I wanted him to be a part of something. "He should at least be with his family. Maybe not Virginia, but the rest of them," I insisted.

The unfeeling, uncaring shadow of a ghost lifted her head. "Ellis has renounced his family."

"He'd never," I protested. Although after tonight, I could see why he might.

The ghost gazed down the lonely path. "He broke ties with his parents, and it broke him as well."

"I see," I whispered.

"Technically, his arguments were in the right," the ghost mused. "But happiness doesn't care about technicalities."

I followed him to a stop a little ways off the path, right in front of a headstone flanked by two spindly red maple trees. He didn't speak, but his shoulders shook as he stood in front of a lonely grave.

Had his father finally worked himself to death?

I stepped next to him to be with him, even if he couldn't see me.

Maybe he could feel me.

And then I saw the name on the headstone.

Beauregard Buford Wydell

Beloved Son and Brother

Taken From Us Too Soon.

I couldn't have been more shocked if lightning had struck me. "No," I said. "No, this can't be true."

"This is the future," the ghost said, implacable.

"Beau is—" *Alive,* I wanted to say. Full of terrible ideas and even worse art, but a force to be reckoned with, and at least he was trying to find himself. "What happened?" I asked, unable to look away from the cold, impersonal tombstone.

"Alcohol poisoning." The ghost's voice went even deeper. "Ellis gave up on everyone in his family, including his younger brother. Without him, the family fell apart. His brother fell apart."

"Surely Ellis doesn't blame himself," I said, looking up into his cold, dark eyes.

He did.

Of course he did. Ellis saw it as his moral imperative to take care of everyone and everything. It was what made him such a great police officer. It was what made him the wonderful man I knew. And if I had any part in pulling him away from his family... No. I wouldn't. That would be terrible.

I watched Ellis drop to one knee and lay the lily on Beau's grave. His long fingers brushed his brother's cold, carved name, and the sob he'd been holding inside burst from him. He buried his face in his arms and wept helplessly, and my heart ached with how tight I wanted to hold him, how badly I wanted to set things right.

"I should be here with him," I sobbed. "I will. Even if we break up, I'll come here with him," I vowed.

The ghost somehow turned without moving at all, the intensity of her power focused squarely on me. "You weren't invited. He wouldn't have taken comfort from the person you became."

It hit me like a mallet. "I stopped giving people chances."

I mean, Virginia deserved to be put at arm's length, but somehow I'd also lost all sympathy for Ellis's mother as a person.

The ghost loomed between me and Ellis. "You were happy about his mother's downfall. You became wrong for him."

As if she were somehow his protector. "Who are you to tell me that?" I challenged.

The ghost's face swirled in a mist beneath the dark hood. "I watch over this family, and I know what they can be."

"So do I." I'd seen it tonight, both the good and the bad. I'd seen it in myself and in them. Yes, Virginia needed to be put in her place—and probably would again even after tonight. I was done taking her abuse lying down. But that wasn't the end of it. "I have to find a way to stand strong and also be a part of Ellis's life and family," I realized.

The ghost stared me down.

"I also have to put a check on my own pride." It was one thing to not put up with Virginia, but to hate her or wish ill on her—it had begun to harm me as a person. I was raised better than that. "I've helped ghosts come together. I've helped the living. Now I just need to do that for myself and the Wydells."

"It's too late," the ghost stated, as if I had no choice in the matter, as if the future were out of my hands entirely.

"You showed me a vision," I said. "But I control the future."

The ghost gazed back to Ellis bent over the grave. It might be the spirit of the family, a guardian or a long-lost ancestor, but I was a girl with a knack for shaking things up.

There was no way I could sit back and let anything bad happen to Ellis, to Beau, to his entire family. Not when I could do something about it. That didn't have to mean bending to

Virginia. And it also didn't mean changing who I was. It just meant I had to conjure up a little holiday miracle using my own personal brand of magic.

I clenched my hands into fists and stared right into the dark oval where the ghost's face wasn't. "I can change it, and I *will*."

12

I barely felt the ghostly whirlwind that delivered me back to the cider mill. I was filled with purpose, and I couldn't stop thinking about what I could do, who I could be.

When my stinging eyes adjusted, I found myself surrounded by rotting apples, rumbling bears, and a rescue that was about to go very, very wrong.

"Verity," Frankie called. "Now! You've got to get the pulley out of the way *now*." The rope had dwindled to a thread and I could hear his naked fear. "Don't make me watch them die."

"Never," I vowed. "You," I said to the faceless ghost of Christmas future. "Thank you. You've helped me more than I could ever have imagined. More than I probably realize." I'd dwell later. "Now do you think you can handle a quick rescue operation in the real world?"

The ghost's faceless visage swirled under her hood. "I keep my promises."

Good. I gestured at the hook and pulley, whose rotation was gaining speed as the last strands of rope feathered away.

"We need to move that machinery away from the hole in the floor."

"Step back," the ghost murmured, her gaze locked on the shaking pulley. And then she began to spin. As she did, she grew smaller. The gray of her cloak folded in on itself, tighter and tighter until she looked like a dense thunderhead, crackling with energy.

"Holy smokes," Hale whistled.

"Told you she was powerful," Phineas said, drawing closer to Hale.

The gray swirling ghost flowed over the pulley and hook and, instead of pushing on them, she completely encompassed them. She inched toward us, and slowly, surely, the hook moved with her.

"What the hell is that thing?" Frankie demanded from the hole.

I didn't know. But she was on our side.

Belatedly I realized that I needed to get out of the way. Pronto. I stepped back until I was almost up against the door. All the hairs on my arms stood up on end, responding to the static charge in the air. I'd never felt a ghost do this before. I'd felt them cold and creepy, numbing and terrifying, but I'd never felt something so raw and elemental.

The hook and pulley inched my way.

"Just a few feet more," I pleaded, as if wanting could make it so. The hook and pulley were still over the hole. Their combined weight had to be hundreds of pounds. The ghost appeared to be slowing down.

"Oh!" The strands making up the remnants of the rope began to unravel so fast they appeared to evaporate. Moving the pulley was one thing. Supporting that massive weight once the rope was completely gone was something else. But I couldn't launch myself over the hole. I couldn't catch it. "Help her!"

With a curse, Hale surged forward, joining the lightning ball and coalescing around the rope.

Phineas rushed in behind him. I heard him cry out before melding into the energy storm.

The fraying slowed, but didn't stop, and the hook still had two more feet to go before it reached the questionably solid ground of the upper floor.

"Frankie!" I gasped.

"I see it!" he hollered.

I pointed at the mass of ghosts. "We need you!"

"I don't know those people," he pleaded. "I'm not merging energy with them!"

"Frankie, please," I implored. "Do it for the bears."

He rose out of the hole, his mouth working but no words coming out. He looked down at the cubs and clenched his jaw. "Hold on, kiddos!" He rose and allowed himself to be sucked into the mass of swirling ghosts.

It surged and spun, swallowing him whole.

The hook and pulley crept closer to the floor at the edge of the hole...closer...*closer...*

But it didn't make a difference.

The rope snapped with the hook still at least a foot from safety. I gasped as the whole thing started to fall. We were too late!

I braced for impact, for tragedy, when suddenly, the hook and pulley caught in midair.

The cloud of energy blazed red underneath it, and with a sound like a screaming swarm of bees, the entire contraption spun sideways and shot straight for me, landing with a thud on the wooden floor less than a foot away. Broken bits of wood skittered to land at my toes.

The boards groaned under my feet, but they held.

I stared, too shocked to utter a word.

The red cloud dissipated with a whoosh and a release of pressure, and three groggy ghosts—only three—materialized in front of me. A breathless Phineas, a bent-over Officer Hale, and Frankie, who collapsed straight through the floor.

"Frankie?" I rushed over to the hole and located him lying on the ground not far from the mama bear, among the discarded apples and debris. The three babies rushed to him, and he didn't even bother to move as they greeted him, dancing through his chest and face.

"You tykes okay?" he muttered, raising a weak hand to his forehead. They tried to nuzzle him in answer, and he grinned.

He was going to have quite the heroic tale to tell Molly. And if he didn't brag on himself, I would.

I turned to Phineas and Hale. "How are you two doing?"

"I hadn't been planning on my own adventure tonight," Phineas said, double-checking to see if he was still in one piece. He was. "I was certain that I would be completely drained of energy after such an immense task, but..."

"She took the brunt of it," Officer Hale said, straightening, cracking his back as he searched for the powerful ghost who had helped us all tonight. But she was nowhere to be found. "I don't know who she used to be when she was alive, but I think I would have been scared of her."

"She certainly got her way," I said. She'd broken through to me. She'd made me realize the part I had to play in Ellis's family, should I choose to adjust my attitude. And she'd helped us too. Donna would be happy to know the animals were safe. "Thank you, guys," I said to Phineas and Hale. "I'm glad I saw what I saw, even though some of it scared the bejeebers out of me."

"The question is, what will you do now, Miss Long?" Phineas asked.

"I'm going to make it better." I wouldn't apologize. I wouldn't backtrack. But I would blaze a new path for myself and for the family. "I'm going to figure out how to bring the Wydells together as a real family for Christmas."

Phineas smiled broadly. "That's exactly what I hoped you'd say." The door behind him opened with a slow creak, startling me. "It was all I needed to hear. I have been pleased beyond all measure by your company tonight, Miss Long, and even more impressed with your determination."

"Not like you gave her much of a choice," Frankie muttered. The gangster rose through the floor as Phineas faded away. "Can we at least visit those kiddos from time to time?" he asked, taking one last look at the bears.

"We can," I promised. Although I'd most likely stay in the car.

I turned to Hale. "It was so good to see you."

"Merry Christmas, Verity," he said as he began to disappear as well.

"I'll see you at the Christmas party later?" I called after him.

"Not without Frankie's power," he teased, and then he was gone.

Did that mean the extended Wydell family hadn't left Montgomery's home yet? I hoped so. It would make what I needed to do a lot easier to have more people than just Ellis, Beau, and Virginia around.

I checked my watch. "Twenty minutes until Molly arrives."

"We'd better book it," Frankie agreed.

He headed through the wall out toward the car, and I used the door, formulating a plan along the way.

I needed to remind the Wydells what Christmas was all

about: family, friends, love, and acceptance. I needed to remind them that they were better together than apart, that the family could evolve in different directions but keep a strong foundation. I needed to give them something tangible to hold onto, to talk about and enjoy together.

Actually, I had just the thing.

13

We returned home and I straightened Frankie's icicle lights.

"The aspic salad still looks good," he called from inside his shed, as if his masterpiece would somehow fall apart without him.

"I'm so happy for you," I told him, stepping back. His lights looked gorgeous. And Molly would be thrilled to see him, no matter what he served. "Merry Christmas," I called, heading into the house.

"Hey," Frankie called after me, leaning his head out the door. "Merry Christmas to you too, kid."

If I hadn't believed in miracles before, I did now.

I dashed for the house. No sense wasting time. Not when I had a little work to do before heading to what remained of the Wydells' party.

Lucy was thrilled when I walked in the door. She'd been sleeping—the right side of her fur was mushed up from curling into the blankets on my futon. I picked her up and stroked her.

"We did it, sweetie," I said, burying my nose in her soft fur. "We did good." And we were going to do even better.

My pickle appetizer sat on the mantel where I'd forgotten it. Ruined. But that was all right. It took about ten minutes to prep a replacement dish for the party and twenty minutes to bake it, which gave me enough time to head upstairs and rinse away the dirt and cobwebs from my hair. I slipped on black ballet flats and picked out a dress I loved, a simple sleeveless holly-green shift that was both cute and comfortable. I applied a glossy coat of pale pink lip gloss, settled my grandmother's filigree cross right above my heart, and smiled at my reflection.

There you are.

My cast-iron pan was piping hot when I took it out of the oven, so I added a pair of elbow-length oven mitts to my ensemble. I loaded up a basket with some holiday essentials and tucked it onto the passenger seat, with the pie on the floor, then steered down the drive toward the property I'd left not too long ago.

Only when I stood in front of Montgomery Wydell's front door did I stop to wonder if this was a good idea.

Time to find out. I placed the basket at my feet, adjusted the warm pan in my hands, and took a deep breath, inhaling the sweet, spicy scent of my last-minute dessert. Then I knocked on the door with my elbow.

No one answered.

It was fairly quiet inside, and the lace curtains over the windows obscured my view, but there were still plenty of cars parked in front of the house. Surely someone had to hear me. Maybe they were just stunned into immobility by the idea that anyone would willingly walk in there right now.

Well, I was ready to be part of the Wydell family Christmas, and I wasn't going away. I would stand and knock on that door until someone opened it up or until Christmas Day, whichever came first.

I was only one person, and far from universally liked at that, but I was going to do my darnedest to remind the Wydells what they were to each other, what they should be. What they had been. I straightened my back and prepared to knock on the door with my knee if I had to, but the door swung open just before I attempted that particular balancing act.

Ellis stood framed by the warm light of the sitting room, his eyes wide as he stared at me. I didn't think I'd ever seen him so surprised. "You came!" He sounded immensely gratified, and if the way he was eyeing my dress was any indicator, I'd pretty much knocked his socks off. I smiled at him, and he stepped forward and tilted my chin up for a kiss. His mouth tasted like honey bourbon and hot chocolate, and I almost forgot the dish I was holding.

"Merry Christmas," I murmured to him after we parted a little.

"Merry Christmas to you, too. Look, I'm so sorry for earlier," he began, but I cut that off with a shake of my head.

"It's all right," I said. "I've done some thinking."

"Oh no," he said, as if any thinking when it came to his family was a very bad idea indeed.

"It's good," I assured him. It was for us, at least. "Is everyone still here?" I asked as he retrieved my basket from the porch and escorted me inside.

"They are," he said, leading me into the party.

Beau was the first to recognize me. He shot up from the loveseat, and it took me a moment to shake off the déjà vu. The scene appeared exactly like I remembered it from the vision with Officer Hale.

"Good to see you." Beau walked to me, a champagne glass

held loosely in one hand. "Ellis said you weren't going to make it."

"Plans change," I told him, glad to see him whole and mostly well. "Merry Christmas, Beau." I leaned in and gave him a warm one-armed hug. "Do you mind grabbing this for me?" I asked, holding out my delectable dessert, giving him a whiff.

"Oh, sure, let me just—um—" He juggled the champagne glass like he'd forgotten it was there.

"I can take that," Ellis said, lifting it right out of Beau's hand.

Beau was so busy getting a good grip on my dessert he didn't notice Ellis pouring his drink out into a potted fern. He sniffed at the edge of the tinfoil covering the pan. "This smells amazing. Kind of familiar." He studied me. "Have you made this before?"

"This is the first time," I said, directing Ellis to set the covered basket next to the loveseat, almost underneath the Christmas tree. "Come on. You have to taste it," I said, walking with the brothers into the party and straight to the dessert table.

"What is it?" Ellis asked, dodging around Beau, trying to lift the foil.

"It's an old family recipe," I said as Beau set it on the table. I eased the foil from the top, and the scent of freshly baked pear pandowdy filled the air.

I hadn't been sure about substituting pears for apples at first, but the dish smelled absolutely divine. The fruit was soft and steeped in spices—including cardamom—and the biscuit topping had turned a beautiful golden brown.

"Oh my God." Beau looked dumbfounded, and Ellis wasn't far off. "This looks exactly like Grandma Dottie's apple pandowdy."

I'd seen a Dottie at the cider mill earlier. "Was Dottie's mother named Charlotte?" I asked.

"Yes," Beau said, surprised.

Ellis closed his eyes for a moment, clearly remembering. "We haven't had pandowdy since Grandma Dottie passed fifteen years ago." He cracked an eye open and—oh, there was the smirk. "Who have you been talking to?" he asked quietly as Beau began calling over the old-timers.

Thank goodness none of them had left yet.

"I'll tell you all about it later," I said, sparing a wink for Ellis. And I would. I'd tell him all of it—the good, the bad, even the scary. It was past time to talk honestly with each other. We owed each other that.

"I'm glad you made it." Montgomery's wife, Susan, bustled over and treated me to a warm hug even though I hadn't seen her in two years. "You're always welcome here," she assured me.

"This had better not be your surprise," Virginia said from across the kitchen.

"Ignore her," said Jimmy, placing a hand on the kitchen table and shoving himself up on his cane. He walked straight past Virginia to us. "I've missed you, kid," he said to me with a grin. "You remember my wife, don't you?" he asked, making room for Great-Aunt Flora. She was a round, white-haired woman whose light-up red and green sweater made her look a bit like a Christmas tree ornament.

"It's so nice to see both of you," I said. "It's been too long."

"That it has," Jimmy said, taking my hands in his.

"Stop buttering her up just to get a bigger slice of dessert," Montgomery joked, cutting in. "Is that a pandowdy you brought with you?"

"It sure is," I told them.

"It smells just like my mother's," he said, delighted.

"If only we'd gotten the recipe from Charlotte before she died," Flora tsked. "Your sister made a good imitation, but it wasn't quite the same."

"Grab the forks," Jimmy urged.

"This one is made with pears," I said as a grateful Susan began serving up dessert to the growing crowd.

Virginia remained across the room, glaring at us. Well, that was her choice. She could isolate herself if she wished. I was eager to try Charlotte's signature dessert.

Jimmy took a big bite and pretended to lose his feet in ecstasy. "It tastes just like my mom's."

"I don't know how you did it," Montgomery said, closing his eyes as he chewed. "Charlotte took that recipe to the grave with her."

"I remember that smell," Ellis's father said, hanging up the phone and wandering toward the table.

"Have some," I said, smiling at him.

"Thanks." He took a plate, and for the first time in years, he looked me in the eye.

Virginia stared a hole in his back as he took a large bite. "Verity Long," he muttered appreciatively, chewing, "What have you done?"

We'd see.

White wrinkles emerged at the corners of Virginia's crimped mouth. "And pears, what a great idea," Leland enthused. "Grandma Charlotte used to make this with apples."

"It's just as good," Uncle Jimmy agreed.

"Well, I happened to have a lot of pears on hand," I said, sparing a grin for Virginia.

"What else have you got in there?" Susan asked, cutting more, passing out plates.

"Oh, the usual. Sugar, cinnamon, cloves," I mused. "And a secret ingredient or two."

Jimmy seemed to be smiling despite himself. "Is that right?"

"A secret ingredient!" Flora crowed, poking her husband gently in the side. "Lord, she sounds just like Charlotte, don't she? If you can cook like her, we're lucky to have you here!"

"We are, indeed. Where have you been all night?" Jimmy asked.

I couldn't exactly explain what had happened earlier with Virginia, not if I wanted to make this a happy holiday. Surprisingly, Beau was the one to step in and help me out. "Verity's got family in town, Uncle Jimmy, and lots of friends too," he explained, as charming as ever. "Her time is valuable."

"Let me guess: time is money?" Jimmy sighed and shook his head. "Where have I heard that before."

"Probably from me," Beau said frankly. "Because sometimes I'm an idiot. But what I mean is, Verity is valued by a lot of people, and she works hard to make time for them all. Even when some of us don't deserve it."

Aww. I would have hugged him again if he wasn't hovering over his dessert like he thought someone might steal it from him.

Ellis gently hip-checked his brother. "Get out of the way so I can get another piece."

"Work around me."

"I will work right *through* you if I have to."

"Boys, boys." Virginia strolled toward our happy crowd, a wintry smile pasted on her lips. "Do try to act like the adults you should be. And Verity." If looks could kill, I'd already be six feet under. "Here you are."

"Here I am," I agreed. I wouldn't apologize, but I would include her if she wished. "Would you like some pear pandowdy? I feel like you should get a serving, since I couldn't have made it without you."

Virginia shook her head. "Unlike some people here, I have a care for my figure." She glanced down into the pan with a faint sneer. "Only you could turn those elegant pears into a lumpy dessert."

Uncle Jimmy, who'd taken a second plate for himself, scooped a bite into his mouth with a sound of pure satisfaction. "Who cares how it looks, when it tastes like this?" he said after he swallowed. "This is amazing. Delicious. Miss Verity, let me shake your hand on a job well done."

Uncle Jimmy's seal of approval seemed to change the mood of the party. Between the pandowdy and the special cider Susan dredged up from the basement to go with the family recipe, people were finally gathered together around the table.

"It really does go best with cider," Montgomery said, toasting an elder uncle as the crowd stood eating and exchanging stories between bites. I listened, satisfied, as they reminisced about the last time they'd had something like this, the way Charlotte used to guard her recipes, and, "Oh, do you remember her roast beef? What about her scalloped potatoes? Do you remember the huge tray of those she used to make when we got together at the old mill? The cider mill! Is it even standing anymore?"

It was.

I was starting to think that cider mill was the heart and soul of the Wydell family—or at least a place where they could start to remember how close the family used to be.

"If it's still there, you young ones should have a bonfire out there sometime," Montgomery suggested.

"I think we all should," I suggested. "Maybe in the spring." Once the bears moved on.

I stood next to Ellis in the center of it all, enjoying the fruits of my labor.

"What changed?" he asked, still trying to put it together.

"Nothing. Everything," I told him.

Virginia had retreated all the way back to the door of the kitchen, deliberately aloof. She appeared absolutely thunderstruck when her husband, Leland, walked up and offered her a plate of pear pandowdy. "Come on. Try it," he urged her. "I remember once when I was little and I got sick, this was all I would eat."

"I'm sorry for you and your childhood," Virginia said, wrinkling her nose.

"It's tasty," Leland said, trying again. "Mother got Grandma Charlotte to come over twice that week and make it for us." He smiled slightly. "I think they used it as an excuse to get together, honestly."

"I remember that too," Montgomery piped up. "I made Mama bring me with her so we could play, and I ended up catching your chicken pox. And we both had to wear those awful—"

"Mittens!" Leland said, abandoning Virginia. "So we wouldn't scratch ourselves raw! Only they were made of wool, and good lord, that made the itching even worse." The two men broke into hearty laughter while Ellis and Beau stared at their dad like they'd never met him before. Apparently, this was a side of him they didn't see often.

"Hmph." A glass of cider appeared in front of me. I turned to accept it with thanks, then almost dropped it when I realized it was *Virginia* holding it out to me. Oh God. Had she had time to poison it?

"I suppose," Virginia said, drawing out the *pose* a bit so that it came off more dubious-sounding, "your dish must taste far better than it looks for Leland to be interested."

"People do seem to like it," I said neutrally.

"It would probably have gone over even better if you had bothered to arrive on time."

"Ah, but then I couldn't have had the fun of telling you off," I said and took a sip of my cider—cold and bracing. It really was delicious. "By the way, you owe me one hundred and seventy dollars."

She stared openly at me and I let her.

"Oh, what the heck," I said, waving her off. "Forget it. Money comes and goes."

"Since when have you not worried about that?" she demanded.

"There are more important things," I said, lifting my glass. "Merry Christmas, Virginia."

Mouth tight, she spun on her heel and walked away.

"I think that went pretty well," I said to myself and took another sip of cider.

I couldn't have a conversation with Virginia without her making at least one attempt to draw blood. But it didn't matter, not right now. Virginia was not the entire Wydell family, and as long as the rest of them wanted me around, then I was going to be there. They were too important to the people I loved for me to let them go, and I knew now that I could make a place for myself with them.

I didn't have a chance to get off my feet for another hour, I was so busy socializing.

"Aunt Flora and Aunt Susan both want you to write down that recipe," Ellis said, at last whisking me away to the loveseat.

We sat down together, and I leaned my head against Ellis's shoulder while he put his arm around me. "I'll have to ask Charlotte if it's all right."

"I knew it," he said, trailing a hand through my hair. "Thanks, Verity."

"I'm glad it worked out. Glad to be here." But tired, too. Hiking to the cider mill, fumbling around in the dark next to four bears, and going on three different ghostly journeys was finally catching up to me.

"This is the longest any of the aunts and uncles have stayed at this party in almost a decade, I think. You brought some magic with you tonight."

"I had help," I told him.

"And I want to know all about that, but first, what's in the basket?"

"Oh!" I reached over the edge of the seat and lifted the basket onto my lap. I drew back the scarf I'd used to cover it and showed him Lucy, curled up and snoring contentedly, one paw hugging a slice of half-eaten pear.

"You brought a skunk to the party." He laughed.

"I can't wait to show your mother," I joked, but in all seriousness, "I couldn't leave her home alone, not when she could celebrate Christmas with us," I explained. "And I knew she'd be too exhausted from meeting her idol to do much more than sleep."

Ellis raised an eyebrow. "Her idol?"

"Donna Lankin stopped by earlier tonight. She's the lady who helped me save Lucy." I stroked a single finger down the bridge of Lucy's nose, then chuckled when she drowsily covered her whole muzzle with her paws. "She changed my life," I said. "They both did."

"You and Lucy suit each other," Ellis said. "She's a brave choice for a pet, but then you're one of the bravest people I know." He nodded toward the food table, where Virginia was stiffly, but willingly, helping Beau gather plates. "Case in point."

I smiled at him. "She is who she is, and I accept that. But it goes both ways. I'm going to be exactly who I am as well—in this case, a girl who didn't want to leave her skunk out of the party on Christmas Eve."

A sudden movement drew my attention to the window. At first I thought maybe a gust of wind had caught a white shutter, but there was no banging noise. There *was* something white, though—or actually, some*one*. Donna stood just outside the house, and as soon as she saw me notice her, she waved again.

"Speak of the devil." Or an angel was more like it. "She's here." I covered Lucy up and got to my feet, bringing Ellis with me. "I'd love for you to meet her."

"It'd be my pleasure." He nodded. Although he couldn't see her or speak to her, a couple of ghost hunters on our last adventure had given us a spectral communication app that sometimes worked. Ellis patted down his pants pockets. "Looks like I left my phone in my jacket, so you'll have to translate for me."

I never minded.

"This way." I led him into the formal dining room, around the kitchen, and finally out to the mudroom, which had a door that led to the back porch. We stepped outside, and goose bumps rose on my arms and legs.

"Oh, honey!" Donna exclaimed. "You did it! You saved the babies and their mama, too. Oh, I could just kiss you!"

"I was glad to do it, although a little warning about what I was getting into would have been nice." Ellis appeared a tad perplexed. "I'll explain soon," I promised him. I made introductions and passed along greetings, and I might have done more if a loud crash hadn't just sounded from inside the kitchen.

Ellis frowned. "I'd better go see if I can help. Please ask your friend to excuse me. I hope we can talk more next time."

I nodded. "I'll be in shortly," I assured him. He walked away, and Donna chuckled.

"I hate to see him leave, but I love to watch him go," she

said wistfully.

"Donna!" I pressed a mock-scandalized hand to my chest.

"Well, honey, I might be dead, but that doesn't mean I'm *dead.* I won't keep you, but I wanted to make sure everything went all right."

"It did, although really, about the bears—"

"Oh, that mama was sleeping good. It's not like moving a pulley makes a lot of noise. Took less than a minute, right? Just so long as you didn't try to invade her space downstairs. Or wake her or her cubs." Donna laughed, as if the thought were inconceivable.

"Yes, that would be suicidal," I agreed.

In the distance, in the direction of the orchard, I saw the flutter of a familiar ghost. Phineas. He tipped his hat to me again before fading from view.

Donna smiled at his evaporating figure and gave him a mock salute.

"Wait. Were you two working together?" I asked.

"I swear we didn't manufacture that crisis to get you involved," Donna promised. "It was a way of killing two birds with one stone, that's all. I'm not blind to the needs of my fellow man any more than I'm blind to the needs of animals. Animals are just easier to help."

Maybe that was true, but tonight she'd helped make a positive change for a lot more than the local wildlife. "Thank you," I said, from the very bottom of my heart. "For everything."

Donna had put me in the position to save the heart of the man I loved, to salvage the Christmas spirit of a family in need, and to hang on to my own happiness. It had all started with Lucy, but my skunk was just the beginning. A little Christmas miracle, one of many I'd been given. And on this Christmas, as well as every other day to follow, I would be thankful.

NOTE FROM ANGIE FOX

Thanks so much for decking the halls and raising a glass with Verity and the gang this holiday season. I've been wanting to go back to Sugarland for Christmas, even if there is a trash can to be decorated and a Jell-O salad to be saved. (Okay, now Frankie is pinging me to insist that aspic is delicious. And to his credit, from what I hear, Jell-O salads really were *the* thing in the 1930's. Cookbooks of the day assumed you had a mold and knew how to use it!)

The next book in the series is called *Southern Bred and Dead*. In it, Frankie confronts his killer, while Verity and Ellis work through the stunning revelation Verity overheard in *The Mint Julep Murders*. It's never a dull day in Sugarland!

If you are interested in receiving an email each time Angie releases a new book, please sign up at www.angiefox.com. You'll receive a happy note from me on release day, and in the meantime, your information will be kept safe by Lucy and a pack of highly-trained guard skunks.

Thanks for reading!

Angie

ABOUT THE AUTHOR

New York Times and *USA Today* bestselling author Angie Fox writes sweet, fun, action-packed mysteries. Her characters are clever and fearless, but in real life, Angie is afraid of basements, bees, and going up stairs when it's dark behind her. Let's face it: Angie wouldn't last five minutes in one of her books.

Angie earned a journalism degree from the University of Missouri. During that time, she also skipped class for an entire week so she could read Anne Rice's vampire series straight through. Angie has always loved books and is shocked, honored, and tickled pink that she now gets to write books for a living. Although, she did skip writing for a week this past fall so she could read Victoria Laurie's Abby Cooper psychic eye mysteries straight through.

Angie makes her home in St. Louis, Missouri with a football-addicted husband, two kids, and Moxie the dog.

If you are interested in receiving an email each time Angie releases a new book, please sign up at www.angiefox.com.

Also be sure to join Angie's online Facebook community where you will find contests, quizzes, general silliness, and special sneak peeks of new books.

From New York Times *Bestselling Author, Angie Fox, the first book in the* USA TODAY *bestselling* Southern Ghost Hunter *series*

Southern Spirits

When out of work graphic designer Verity Long accidentally traps a ghost on her property, she's saddled with more than a supernatural sidekick—she gains the ability see spirits. It leads to an offer she can't refuse from the town's bad boy, the brother of her ex and the last man she should ever partner with.

Ellis Wydell is in possession of a stunning historic property haunted by some of Sugarland Tennessee's finest former citizens. Only some of them are growing restless—and destructive. He hires Verity to put an end to the disturbances. But soon, Verity learns there's more to the mysterious estate than floating specters, secret passageways, and hidden rooms.

There's a modern day mystery afoot, one that hinges on a decades-old murder. Verity isn't above questioning the living, or the dead. But can she discover the truth before the killer finds her?

What Reviewers are saying about *Southern Spirits*

5 Stars! "'Loved' does not begin to describe my feelings for this story."

5 Stars! "I could not put it down (ended up reading all night long midnight till 3am)."

5 Stars! "I loved the heroine because she is gutsy and quirky, definitely not a wilting flower, and I am super excited about where her story is going."

5 Stars! "I fell in love with this series from the first book!"

SOUTHERN SPIRITS

SOUTHERN SPIRITS

Chapter One

I lived in a gorgeous antebellum house. Not too large. Certainly not too small. The white columns out front were tasteful, even though they had chipped in places. The porch was welcoming, if a little weathered. Over the years, my family had sold the estate around the house, piece by piece, so that the sprawling peach orchard and even the grand front drive had given way to tidy bungalows lining the long road to the main house.

Grandma had said it made gossip travel even faster, the way they built houses so close together these days. I always told her that the good citizens of Sugarland, Tennessee, needed no help.

Still, I loved the place.

And I absolutely despised letting it go.

"Anyone home?" my best friend, Lauralee, called from the front of the house. "Verity, are you in here?" She added a few knocks on the front door, out of politeness rather than practicality, since the door already stood open.

We'd endured a stifling hot afternoon, and I couldn't afford to run the air-conditioning. I needed any breeze I could get.

"In the back parlor," I called. "Mourning," I added, since there was nothing left in the once-stately room, save for a cooler filled with ice, my tea jug, and a lopsided futon I inherited from a roommate back at Ole Miss. The pink-papered walls and elegant wood accents appeared so strange without rugs and furniture, like a queen stripped of her jewels.

The estate sale was yesterday and the place had been picked clean. The vultures.

"I'm sorry." Lauralee's voice echoed in the empty room. She let her purse and a cloth grocery sack slip from her shoulder to the floor; then she wrapped an arm around me and squeezed, the curled end of her ponytail tickling my cheek.

I gazed up at the ugly black hole where the crystal chandelier had hung for more than one hundred years. "Thanks." I'd come to terms with this. I really had. I turned and looked her straight in the baby blues. "I'd live in a paper bag if it meant I didn't have to marry that bastard."

My friend drew back and tucked a lock of my hair behind my ear. "Seems like he's trying to make you good on your word."

"True. But I'm not done yet." I refused to even entertain the thought.

This past May, I'd scandalized the town when I jilted the most eligible bachelor in three counties—at the altar, no less. It was a disaster. Two old ladies fainted straight out of the pew reserved for the Southern Heritage Club. Then Beau's own mother collapsed, taking down a lovely hydrangea arrangement. I secretly wondered if Mrs. Leland Herworth Wydell III didn't want to be upstaged, even at her own son's ultimate humiliation.

Truth was, he'd brought it upon himself. But I suppose it was quite shocking if you didn't know the details.

I hadn't told a lot of people. I'd wanted to spare my sister.

Lauralee chewed on her lip as she surveyed what little remained in my home. "Tell me you at least made some decent money yesterday."

"I did." I'd sold everything I could lay my hands on and kept only the absolute necessities, namely my futon, my grandmother's pearl wedding ring, and the quilts she'd made for me. It had hurt like a physical pain. I'd had to remind myself that it was only furniture, clothes. *Stuff.* I still had my health. And my friends. Not to mention my family. I brought a hand to my throat, where I used to wear my grandmother's cross from when she was about my age. The delicate gold and silver filigree antique now belonged to my not-quite-mother-in-law. "I still owe more than twenty thousand dollars."

I gazed across the once-grand, now empty back parlor turned family room. I tried to ignore the hollow place in my stomach. Tomorrow, my ancestral home would go on the market. I let out a ragged sigh. "It's dumb, but I keep hoping for a miracle."

A hidden treasure in the attic. Gold under the stairs. Stranger things had happened, right? All I knew was that I couldn't lose this house. I just couldn't.

Lauralee wrapped an arm around my shoulder and gave me a squeeze. "You'll make it. You always do," she said, in a way that made me think she actually believed it. She took in the fourteen-foot ceilings, the crown moldings. "With the money you have left over from the sale, you can make a fresh go of things."

A new start. I certainly needed *something* to change. And yet...

"I can't believe it's all gone." What had taken more than a century to accumulate had become fractured history in the space of a day. "Except for that," I said, pointing to a god-awful vase on the mantel.

My friend made a face. "I never even noticed that before."

It would have been hard to ignore. "It was in the attic," I explained. "Where it belongs." The green stones that circled the top were sort of pretty, but a crude, hand-painted scene marred the copper exterior and a healthy dent gouged the lower half. The dotty old relic looked completely out of place on an ornate marble mantel with flowers and hummingbirds carved into the corners.

"Yeek." Lauralee crossed the room for a better look. She attempted to lift the monstrosity and then changed her mind. It was heavier than it looked, wider at the top and tapered down to a flared base at the bottom. In fact, it reminded me more of an antique Grecian urn. She turned to me. "Is it a spittoon?"

"I think it's a vase," I said, joining her. "Beau gave it to me. He called it an historic heirloom. Looking back, I think he just needed to get rid of it."

In the beginning of our relationship, Beau had given me heartfelt gifts—a pressed flower from the picnic we took on our first date, a little notebook with one of our private jokes written on the inside cover. Later, it was last-minute gas station flowers.

And objects like this.

"It's hideous," Lauralee said.

"A true monstrosity," I agreed. Or else he would have let me return it when I gave him back the ring. "You want it?" I asked, turning the dented side toward her.

My friend let out a snort. "Not unless I can thunk your ex over the head with it."

I shot her a conspiratorial grin. "You'd do that for me?"

She raised her delicate brows. "Nothing would give me more pleasure," she said in a sweet, Southern tone that would make you think I'd offered mint juleps on the verandah.

"I suppose I could toss it," I said. I still had one trash can left.

She waved me off. "Keep it out. It's a focal piece. The only one you have. Here." She scooted it over toward the pale shadow where my mother's crystal swan used to be. "It'll draw people's eyes to the fireplace instead of that hideous futon."

"Way to remind me that I'm sleeping in the parlor." No way was I going to try dragging a futon up a flight of stairs.

She crossed over to the opposite wall to retrieve her hemp grocery bag from the floor. "Maybe this will help you forget," she said, holding up a bottle of Malbec.

"Mine," I said, on her in an instant. Although I'd have to tell her Beau took the stemware.

She handed me the bottle and the opener, then pulled out a pair of plastic wineglass tops from her bag. "My kids used the bottoms to play flying-saucer frisbee, but I didn't think you'd mind."

I wound the opener into the cork. "Who won?"

"Who knows?" She held out both glasses and I poured.

It was well past cocktail hour in the Old South. In fact, the sun was beginning to set.

"Should we retire to the floor?" I asked, a bit punchy with the unreality of it all.

Lauralee handed me a glass. "We might end up there anyway," she said as we both took a seat.

I smelled lemon polish and old wood as I stretched my legs out over the floor I'd lovingly scrubbed. We leaned our backs against the plaster wall and sipped our wine as the shadows lengthened over the room.

It wasn't like I had any lamps.

"You ever think what might have happened if I hadn't come back home?" I asked her.

I could have gone to the big city after graduating art school. My father died when I was in fifth grade, my mother long since remarried. My sister had bounced around from college to college. I could have found a job at an advertising firm, or at a large company with an in-house graphics department. I wouldn't have been around when Beauregard Buford Wydell decided it was time to take a wife.

This place would have sat empty, but at least it would have stayed mine.

"You belong here, Verity," she said simply, as if it were the only truth.

She had me pegged. I cherished this town and my home. There'd been no other choice for me. Without my roots and my family's heritage, I'd be adrift.

Grandma knew. It was why she left the house to me when she died. The rest of the estate went to my mother, who bought an RV and embraced adventure with my stepfather; and to my sister, who used her portion to pay for her various semesters abroad and half-finished degrees.

But, truly, this place had been mine even before Grandma made it legal.

I took an extra-large sip of wine as Lauralee's phone chimed. She handed me her glass and pulled the smart phone from her back pocket. The glowing screen lit her pixie face and what she saw made her frown.

"Trouble in paradise?" I asked as she checked her text messages.

The faint lines around her eyes crinkled at the corners and

she sighed. "It's Big Tom. Tommy Junior got his head stuck in the hallway banister again."

I should have faked some sympathy, but it happened at least once a month. The kid was forever getting stuck in something. "Do you have to leave?"

"No." She took her wine back from me. "Big Tom has it handled." She held her glass like a diva at a cocktail party. "Heck, if I was home, I'd be calling him. He's better at prying the railings off."

I tried to imagine it and failed. "I'm starting to think you need the wine more than I do." She had four children under the age of seven—all boys.

She gave me the old pishposh as she leaned against the wall. "It's the first two kids that get you. After that, you're broken in."

I'd take her word for it.

A beam of slanting sunlight caught the ugly vase and shone through the dust in the air around it in a way that reminded me of dozens of mini fireflies. The copper itself didn't gleam a bit.

"Oh my God..." Lauralee said, leaning forward, glass in hand. "It's dirty," she said with relish.

"I saw the dust," I told her. I'd give it a good scrubbing before the open house tomorrow.

But she was already halfway to her feet. "No. The painting on it is dirty. As in sexy time."

"No way," I said, practically leaping off the floor to get a look.

"It's so bad it's brilliant." She laughed as I pulled the vase from the mantel. "I don't know why I didn't notice it before. Now that I see it, I can't *not* see it."

"Where?" I asked. Yes, there were some highly styled, almost art-deco swirly bits. They were hard to make out. It looked like people dancing. Maybe.

My friend rolled her eyes. "Has it been that long since you got laid?"

"I plead the fifth," I said as I carried the vase over to a beam of fading sunlight by the window. I traced a finger over the crude painting. Then I saw it—a girl and a boy...and another boy. Now how did that work?

"They're getting lucky," Lauralee said, crowding me to get another look. "It's a lucky vase."

I stifled a snicker. "Can you see Beau's mother displaying this in her parlor? Maybe she knows what the girl is doing with two boys."

"And I think there's a goat," Lauralee added.

"No," I said, yanking it closer to see.

"Made you look." She laughed.

Did she ever.

"Wait till the old biddies see this," I said. And they would. We'd have plenty of gawkers tomorrow.

Lauralee gave me a loving punch to the arm. "You might have to point it out to them. They'll gasp and moan, but they'll secretly love it."

My friend's phone chimed again. She looked, and this time her sigh was heavier. "Rats."

"Trouble?"

She held up her phone to show me a text photo of her five-year-old son sitting next to a pile of debris, grinning. "Hiram got hold of a screwdriver and took apart the hall clock while Tom was working on the banister. I'd better go."

Typical day in the Clementine household. I folded her into a hug. "Thanks for the support."

She squeezed hard. "Thanks for the laugh." She smiled as she pulled back. "I love you, girlie." She tilted her chin down. "And I, for one, am glad you came home."

She was a true friend, and for that I was grateful. "Me too."

~

After she left, I took that vase off the mantel and traced my finger over it. Boy, girl...and that really could be a goat. I smiled to myself. Lauralee was right. I would make it through this, despite Beau and his mother and every damned one of them.

I'd be strong. Free. Maybe not quite as free as those happy fun-time people painted on the vase, but I'd be a new woman all the same. My own woman.

I wet the pad of my thumb and used it to wipe the dust from the rim. As I did, something shifted inside of it. Strange. I lifted the small bronze lid and saw at least three inches of dirt.

Well, no wonder. Nobody had cleaned the thing or showed it any love in ages.

No problem. I'd take it outside and rinse it down with the hose. I could turn the dented spot toward the wall and this little piece of faded glory might pass for something worth buying.

Now would also be a good time to track down Lucy. That sneaky little skunk would spend all night outside terrorizing the neighbors if I'd let her.

I pushed past the screen door and saw she wasn't in her bed out on our sprawling back porch. A walk down the steps showed she wasn't under her favorite apple tree, either—or as she probably thought of it: the place where snacks dropped down from heaven. After a little bit of searching, I found Lucy catching the last bit of sun on the stone pavers lining the rose garden at the back of the house.

As soon as she saw me, she rolled right off the paver and

landed on her back in the grass. She gave a chipper, skunky grunt and waddled over to greet me. I loved the way she walked, with her head down and her little body churning with every step. It was the cutest thing ever.

"Hiya, sweetie pie." I bent down on one knee to greet her. She thrust her entire snout into my palm and then turned her head for easy petting, making husky, purr-like squawks. She had the softest little cheeks. I stroked her there, then down along the neck and between the ears in the way that made her right back leg twitch. "You enjoying your last day at the house?"

An apartment just wasn't going to be the same for Lucy. I'd found a place that accepted exotic pets, but believe it or not, people around here held a certain bias against skunks. It wasn't enough that I'd had little Lucy's scent glands removed. They wanted her to stop being who she was.

Poor baby.

I'd have to make some adjustments as well after we moved. Our new home, The Regal Towers, was basically an old six-family flat down by the railroad tracks. So close, in fact, that the windows rattled every time a train went by. The doors were made of plywood. I wasn't even sure that was legal, not that management cared. Morton Davis, slumlord extraordinaire, had offered to save it for me on account of the fact we'd attended grades K through eight together at Stonewall Jackson Elementary. I knew it was available because no one else wanted it.

There had to be a way out of this.

Lucy snuggled up to me and tried to climb my leg to get closer.

"You want to help?" I asked, making sure I reached clear of Lucy as I dumped the contents of the vase over Grandma's rosebushes. She gave the little pile a sniff and sneezed.

"You said it." The dirt was loose and dry, which I was glad to see. I'd heard that sort of thing was good for the roots.

It certainly couldn't hurt.

When the last of the fine dust had settled out of the air, I hosed out the vase and poured the water on the roses. They needed it. I'd been neglecting them lately.

"How do you like that?" I asked my climbing vines.

A chilly breeze whipped straight up my spine and shot goose bumps down my arms. It startled me, and I dropped the vase. Lucy darted away.

"Nice work, butterfingers," I mumbled to myself, retrieving it. I spotted a stubborn patch of dirt down in the base and rinsed it out again, but the stuff wouldn't budge.

The rosebushes shuddered. It had to be the wind, but this time, I didn't feel it.

For the first time, I felt uncomfortable in my grandmother's garden.

It was a strange feeling, and an unwelcome one at that. "It's getting late," I told myself, as if that would explain it.

Quick as I could, I reached for the rose snippers I kept under the hose. I cut a full red bloom, with a stem as thick as my finger, and popped it into the vase with a dash of water. Then I hurried back toward the house, careful not to spill a drop.

"Lucy," I called, half-wondering if the skunk wasn't the source of the strange rustling in the rosebushes behind me. "Come on, girl."

She came running from her hiding place under the porch. Something had scared her, too.

The house had never been what you'd call ordinary. We had fish in the pond, each one big as a cat; more often than not, I found fireflies in the attic.

But this was unusual, even for my ancestral home. I didn't like it at all.

Especially when the windows rattled.

"What the hey, girl?" I asked Lucy. And myself.

She turned around and headed back under the porch. Darn it all. She tended to snuggle under my covers at night and I didn't want her all dirty.

You have no idea how hard it is to give a skunk a bath.

A low creaking came from inside the house. The hair on my arms stood on end. Perhaps Lucy was the smart one after all. Unfortunately, there wasn't room under the porch for me.

Instead, I took the steps slowly and crossed the threshold into the darkened kitchen.

My eyes strained against the shadows. Not for the first time, I wished I'd kept at least one light. With shaking fingers, I lit the big, orange, three-wicked candle I'd been using for the last few days.

The house stood still, quiet as a grave. Almost as if it were waiting.

"Is it you, Grandma?" I asked on a whisper. "Are you mad I'm selling?"

If she'd been watching down on me at all—and I knew she did—Grandma would understand I'd been given no choice in the matter.

"Oh no," said a ghostly male voice. "You're staying put, sweetheart." With shock and horror, I realized it was coming from the vase. I dropped it.

The door slammed closed behind me. The bolt clicked, locking on its own as the vase spun and rattled to a stop on the floor.

A chill swept the room. I retreated until my back hit solid wood. I'd never seen a ghost or heard a ghost although I watched *Ghost Adventures* on television and I certainly believed in them and sweet Jesus I was trapped.

I couldn't feel my fingers, or my limbs for that matter. My entire body had gone ice cold. "What do you want?" I asked, voice shaking. Seeing as I hadn't dropped dead on the spot from a heart attack, this had better well be my salvation. "Why are you here?"

The voice laughed, as if it were honest-to-God amused. "I'm here because you chiseled me, princess."

Made in the USA
San Bernardino, CA
11 December 2019

61277420R00095